Marta Traba

MOTHERS AND SHADOWS

translated by Jo Labanyi

readers international

ISBN 0-930523-15-6 hardcover
ISBN 0-935023-16-4 paper cover

FOR GUSTAVO AND ELBA,

LEST WE FORGET

I

The doorbell made her jump. She wasn't expecting anyone and her initial impulse was not to move till the person at the door went away. It might easily be a salesman, or someone who had got the wrong address. But supposing it was someone with news for her? She appealed to the familiar objects around her for reassurance. The bell rang again, less insistently this time, and she felt that if she didn't get up and go to the door straightaway her nerves would get the better of her. All those years of acting had taught her the art of self-control. She moved slowly and deliberately, trying to recall in what play she'd gone through the same motions and pretended to answer a doorbell, but she couldn't sort out the images that flooded into her head. She found herself facing the door and opened it gingerly. Outside the girl looked up, flinching slightly and tossing her hair back over her shoulder. The two of them stood staring at each other, diametrically opposed, one of them in the full sun and the other in the shade of the hallway. She felt relieved at the thought that the girl's position was more exposed than hers and that she might suddenly melt in all that sunlight. And all that would be left would be the tall, spreading trees, with their unkempt branches swaying over the rooftop. She would have liked to efface the girl's image before she'd had time to recognise her, but she found herself switching on the usual ravishing smile, like a river-mouth inviting people to fling themselves into it. She realised her artful guiles were functioning of their own accord and would produce an automatic response to the sight of the girl dissolving in the light; the thought brought her back to reality and made her focus on the figure standing in front of her. She was surprised to see that, despite the heat, she was wearing an open blazer, with her hands sunk in its pockets. But what was surprising about that? Wasn't that her habitual posture? She had a sudden flash of recognition, and guessed she was probably wiping her sweaty hands against the threadbare flannel. Her eyes moved from the girl's hands to her young, drawn face. If anything she looked younger than before, with her long, lank hair draped over her shoulders. The next step was to give her a kiss, trying to avoid touching those stiff and no doubt greasy strands of hair. It's as if time had stood still, she thought as their cheeks brushed and she sniffed that acrid, long-forgotten odour.

But nothing was forgotten. The girl stammered a few incoherent words as she pushed her inside the hall and steered her to an armchair, as if trying to make everything return to its rightful place. If she turned around, the girl would be able to see she'd put on weight and that her body was no longer as lithe as it had been five years before. It was a petty thought, but she couldn't suppress it. The mechanisms of seduction were taking over again. She backed into the armchair facing the girl and arranged her legs on the green velvet cushions. She was wearing a mauve blouse, delicately offsetting the dark green of the chair; she began to feel better. But then she realised the girl had not the faintest idea what was going through her head; her face, out of the sunlight, was no longer stony-white but was flushed an almost unhealthy shade of pink.

Her silence forces the older woman to take the initiative for the second time, and she extricates herself from the armchair, invites her to take off her blazer (which the girl does in the most clumsy fashion imaginable), goes to hang it on the coatstand in the hall, and from the recess lined with bookcases asks if she'd like a coffee. Without waiting for a reply, she goes straight to the kitchen in the hope of getting the conversation going — it always works in the theatre — by tossing out a few casual questions from the distance of the other room, leaving her free to answer or not, as she pleases. She knows her well enough to be sure she'll be too inhibited to get up and follow her into the kitchen. The ploy of going to the kitchen to make some coffee has the added advantage of giving her time to work out how much the girl is likely to know. She remembers getting a letter — or was it several? — at some point since their meeting. She's bound to have heard about her divorce, her all-too-public appearances, the odd scandal and more than one stage triumph. And some one must have told her about the present situation, or why else would she have come to see her out of the blue? On the other hand, what does she know about the girl's life? Dolores, that's her name. Thank God it suddenly came back to her. And with the name come back the stories of the terrible things she had done to her, which she must avoid at all cost. She vaguely remembers that she brought out a book, quite recently, but the truth is she never bothered to look at it properly when she received it, it's always the same with poetry. And why the hell write poetry anyway? She feels a prick of indignation, which serves to clear her head while she assembles the percolator. She must be careful not to mention children or anything to do with pregnancy; and especially not the fact that her son's wife is pregnant, almost four months pregnant, what's worse. Her head reels at the thought that somewhere in Chile they may be kicking her and stamping on her. Wasn't that how. . .? The conversation is clearly fraught with danger. To her alarm she can feel the ground slipping from under her feet, her poise and self-assurance draining away. What ever made her come into the kitchen? The coffee starts to percolate, spluttering loudly. Why on earth did she have to turn up right now, just when she was trying to fend off memories of the past? But she has no right to feel so angry with the girl meekly in the other room. She puts the coffee-pot and two cups on the tray. No, two mugs would be better. Dolores must be studying the room and is probably thinking all her clutter is disgusting and the colonial angels on the wall are grotesque. She must go to the defence

3

of the world of objects she transports around with her like a shell, rescuing it from the girl's scornful gaze. Anyway, aren't those delicate wooden carvings easier to justify than the limitless cruelty of human beings? Her wobbly hands, which she hasn't been able to steady for the last few days, make her spill a few drops of coffee; she can feel her cheeks burning as she searches for a cloth to wipe the tray clean. All of a sudden she's plunged back into despair and, as she re-enters the sitting-room with the tray, she feels utterly desolate. Her knuckles are white from gripping the silver handles. She can't bear to look at her spotted hands, ridged with thick blue veins: the hands of an old woman.

And yet, as she puts the tray down, her ravishing smile lights up again. But to no avail, for the girl, hearing her come back into the room, has got up and is looking out of the window; her hands sunk in her trouser pockets, she makes some remark about how magnificent the trees are: the monkey-puzzle, the ceiba, the two eucalyptuses. Then when she turns around she ignores her and surveys the walls, the pictures, the carvings, with her usual mobile, absent-minded gaze, looking through the objects as though they were of no importance to her. Finally she sinks into the armchair facing the steaming mugs, her hands still in her pockets, and half-closing her eyes murmurs over and over again how good it feels to be here, how good it feels to be here.

The conversation began to flow. Once she'd got over her shyness, the girl could be a wonderful person to talk to, mainly because she was a responsive, intense listener. The older woman, for her part, was a professional conversationalist. As she juggled with the phrases, strategically positioning the pauses to create the maximum suspense, it occurred to her that during the past two weeks she'd spoken to no one except over the phone, endlessly rehearsing the same topics; how I said goodbye to them at Santiago airport, what would they have done when they heard the news, would they have made for the industrial belts? Or the shanty-towns where they had friends? Would they have gone back to the south of the country? Would they have had time to hide? A single theme with an infinite number of variations that drove her to distraction, particularly when the concerned calls from her family betrayed a note of disapproval. Her husband was also in the habit of ringing her from Atlanta every day, on the dot of eight, the first call of the day. She could no longer be bothered to make the effort to ask him how his business trip was going. She couldn't keep up the pretence that she cared about Antonio's affairs, too bad if he noticed. Her nerves frayed by so many pointless phone calls, she was mentally exhausted and on the verge of hysteria. Her one source of relief was the thought that she was all alone in the house by the sea and that the family could hound her only from a distance.

So far the girl had not said a word about it. In fact she'd said very little about anything, preferring to listen as usual. The older woman lit up a cigarette. Was she so quiet because she couldn't compete with her conversation or because she felt embarrassed to say she knew and that she'd come to offer moral support? Whatever the reason, she felt satisfied with her side of the conversation; she'd told her a series of anecdotes about things that had happened on her last tour, plus a few that had not happened. Her life sounded full and action-packed.

The girl smiled at her from deep in the armchair. She looked satisfied too.

'I've always wondered,' she suddenly asked, 'what on earth you'd do if you failed at something. Would you know how to cope with failure? I don't mean a stage hit or flop. I mean something else; I'm probably not putting it very well.'

The woman tried to help her find the words, but dried up in mid-sentence. The subject galled her.

'I mean,' Dolores started, and fell silent again. 'I mean, you plan something, you spend years and years of your life trying to bring it to fruition, and then it falls to pieces around you.'

'One always anticipates the possibility of things going wrong, no matter how optimistic one is. So you just swallow your disappointment, it's not the end of the world.'

'But do you think things could ever go wrong for you? I get the impression you always play to win.'

She decided to hit back. She wasn't having the conversation taking that kind of turn.

'We all play to win,' she snapped. 'Do you mean to tell me you don't? It'd be crazy to play to lose. I'm convinced that winning or losing has a lot to do with whether or not you really want things to turn out well. It's my firm belief that if you want something, if you throw the whole of yourself into it, if you keep on at it, you'll get it. It's as simple as that.'

She felt like adding 'And if things went wrong for you, you've only yourself to blame; you were heading for disaster before they got their hands on you', but she checked herself in time.

'Give yourself body and soul,' the girl muttered, looking away. 'What a load of shit.'

'What was that you said?' She was annoyed at the quiver in her voice.

'Nothing, I'm sorry,' she hastened to reply, her lean cheeks blushing violently. 'I'm talking to myself, I just can't take that kind of optimism. It sounds hollow to me. Maybe it's not, but that's how it sounds to me. For me, reality is all that counts.'

'But reality is what you make of it, that's the whole point. Or is it something people thrust on you?'

She hesitated before answering.

'Yes, it was thrust on me.'

'But you can't fall for that one. How can you talk like that? It's not a question of being naively starry-eyed, obviously not, but you have to accept that you're responsible for what happens to you, or at least that you play a big part in shaping your life. You can use your energy to get things done. If you don't think like that, you'll sink into the most dreadful apathy.'

In her agitation she'd got up and was striding round the sitting-room. The French windows at the far end of the room looked out on to a terrace, the window opposite gave a view of the ceiba, that improbable-looking, ungainly tree, with its bottle-shaped trunk and clusters of pink flowers.

'OK,' the girl came back at her, 'So what are you doing right now about your son?'

She stopped dead in her tracks, and stared at her blankly. So that was what she'd been getting at. She hadn't expected that blow beneath the belt. Hadn't the conversation kept to the decorous exchange of pleasantries? Obviously not. Young people nowadays weren't interested in making conversation for the sake of it, she should have known that from the start. They were always on the alert, ready to pounce. She had a disheartening vision of a relentless, unpitying world. What had made them so remorseless?

She stood blinking, helpless, in the middle of the room.

'There's nothing I can do. But I promise you he'll get out.'

She heard her mutter under her breath: 'It's completely irrational.'

'Yes, of course it's irrational, thank God. Thank God for that, damn you.'

She was suddenly choked by emotion. But she wasn't going to let herself burst into tears, despite the fact that for the past few days her reflexes had been getting the better of her and acting independently of her will. She quickly reflected that the best way to change the subject was to turn it against Dolores. She'd been unkind and deserved to be punished. No matter how hard she might try to avoid it, she'd force her to talk about herself. Maybe that was what she needed? She began to calm down. Perhaps the poor girl had come because she wanted to confide in her, because she needed to talk to someone; it was getting harder and harder to talk to people in Montevideo. And all she'd done was prattle on and on with her string of silly anecdotes. She decided she'd have to start the conversation again from scratch; the pro-spect of taking back the reins assured her. She almost managed a smile as she asked her how old she was now.

The question took her aback. It was amazing, almost alarming how easily she could be made to blush.

'Twenty-eight. And don't tell me I ought to be optimistic at that age, please. Maybe other young people can. But not us, can't you see that? We're finished and done for.'

She tensed up again. But she was determined to stay in control.

'I don't know who you mean by "we".'

At that Dolores swung round in her chair and looked her straight in the eye for the first time, without smiling or blushing.

'Of course you do. You know perfectly well. By "we" I mean the people you met that fateful day, don't try to tell me you don't remember when you kept on referring to it in all your letters.'

'Two or three letters,' she reflected, struck by a malicious thought. 'She must still be in love with me to have such a clear memory or what were completely ordinary letters.'

'We were banking on winning, don't worry, but it just happened that we lost, there's no other way of putting it. It wasn't a stage performance, I can assure you. They didn't get up and take a bow after they'd been killed. It wasn't like being at the opera, I can assure you of that.'

The older woman looked at her. Strangely, she didn't feel offended, despite her tone of voice. She thought that her hands, still in her trouser pockets, must be clenched. And what if they'd burnt them or ripped her fingernails out? They often did. Idiot, stop letting your imagination run away with you! She stared at the girl's bony hands as she picked up her mug of coffee and couldn't see anything wrong with them. She forced herself to think about other things in order not to let herself be drawn into a tight corner. In such a vulnerable position, she had to defend herself as best she could. By any means, and against all comers. She had to go on believing, against all odds, in the fairytale world of wish-fulfilment. Never mind if it was unconvincing, conventional, clichéd.

All that mattered was to stay inside the storybook with its fairy godmother and happy ending.

Dolores asks where the bathroom is and disappears down the corridor at the other end of the room. Just what I didn't want to happen, because now I'm left on my own and I know what will happen. I've spent too many hours watching the movements of that ocean, which sometimes is wave and sometimes sand, silent and surging, sweeping me away only to suck me down into its swirling undercurrents where I watch the débris floating past, that photograph, for instance, which I can't shake off because it's stuck like a stamp on my arm, an arm so eaten away by the murky waters I don't recognise it as my own. I look at the photograph of the four muses, and for the umpteenth time burst out laughing at the sight of my eldest aunt in the role of Euterpe, despite the fact that the only music she ever knew was the sound of boiling water sterilising the syringes in her sanitorium. Did she ever know who Euterpe was? I prop the photo up so I can see my mother, whom my grandparents, in an inspired gesture, had dressed as Poetry, represented by a somewhat crumpled scroll and a goose quill in her free hand. It's clear that, with the future nurse's lyre and my mother's poetic instruments, the photographer had exhausted the reserves of his studio somewhere in the industrial suburbs of Buenos Aires. The other two sisters he had cast in somewhat sorry roles, and no doubt had to bully them into taking up their positions. My second aunt was pointing arm outstretched towards a backcloth depicting a lake with swans on it; I can see her on her deathbed, lying on a grubby mattress stuffed with the money she'd endlessly pinched and scraped to save. So much for the swan... The third aunt was huddling against a backcloth, her head buried in her hands. Melpomene, perhaps? If so, she remained true to the muse, for a person with a greater talent for turning everyday reality into high drama never existed. What tenement building had they step-ped out of? What squalid room partitioned off by a chintz curtain so their father would have somewhere private to put on his woolly long-johns in the bitter cold? And how had that family ended up in that working-class district in the south of the city? She tried to picture the scene when they'd disembarked in the harbour, her mother still a babe-in-arms, her three sisters crawling and squalling. Had they made their way through the city centre? Did they stop off in the squares to untie the bundle of food they'd knotted in a kerchief in case of need? Why does that silly photograph tell me so little, nothing but lies? That ageing immigrant couple, stuck in that room in the tenement building, dined on orchids in their dreams. Believe in the dream or go under. They handed the motto down to their children and my mother ended up playing the piano at the recitals given by the scholarship holders at the Conservatoire — pity about the change of muse — while the former Euterpe filched handfuls of gold thread from the haberdasher's to embroider the concert pianist's blouse. They didn't produce four muses but they got quite close. Four long-distance runners bearing the Olympic torch. Carry on to the first hurdle, keep going to the second, drop dead at the finishing post: the eternal little house with all the latest gadgets, including the bicycles on which a new generation would pedal its way to university. But at the end of the process, when the ocean is clogged with floating débris, houses, refrigerators, cars, pianos, clothes, all manner of objects, is it fair to reproach them? Is there anything to reproach them for? What right have I to feel resentful if I find myself swimming in the midst of my collection of wood carvings and, as I clutch at a passing wing, instead of wrenching it off and hurling it to the bottom of the sea, I fondle its gilt curls as if it were the golden fleece, I'd fall on my knees if it weren't for the sea buoying me up and for the fact that any minute now Dolores is going to come through the far door and she won't be able to believe her eyes if she catches me praying to a wooden angel. I suspect that that photo of the muses contained some kind of a trap, but what kind? At the same time I feel my grandparents were total innocents. Thrown up exhausted on this alien shore, where did they find the reserves of energy to endure those years of hardship? What's the matter with me, I'm rubbing my frozen hands together! So many faces have passed over my dunes in the last few days. I think that what I see is the sand blowing in the wind, swirling in all directions, and then, when I look carefully, I can see thousands of figures wandering in the desert, I know I should notice they're in rags or naked, sometimes just skin and bone, I know I should look at the ground to see how they trail their children's corpses behind them, and yet I refuse to look or listen or feel, I'm not prepared to admit to the existence of those infinite vistas of death and destruction that have opened up now disaster has touched me. What do I care about Biafra and Cambodia and the seas thick with drowning men? How can such things affect me when my role in life is clearly spelt out: to forge ahead come what may, defending to the last the invisible trap my grandparents set for me. They laboured to erect it, they made sacrifices to cherish and possess it. It's thanks to them I've come out on top and am floating in the sea, I've cultivated my little piece of desert. What right has that wretched girl who's taking an age in the bathroom to come and rake it around? And now I come to think of it, isn't she taking rather longer than she ought? When she got up to ask where the bathroom was she said something. Something like: 'Excuse me, I have to keep going to the toilet all the time, that's another little souvenir they left me with.' Again I think what right has she got to expel me from the photograph my grandparents had taken, but my irritation gives way to concern that something unpleasant might be happening to her. Perhaps they burst her bladder? She'd been told that the only reason her spleen had survived was because they'd preferred to stamp on her protruding belly. I press my hands together tightly, there's no way I can get them warm. Once more I feel on the verge of tears, though this time I don't know whether it's on my behalf or hers. Here she is again, she looks perfectly composed, does she have to carry around a tube and a little rubber bag to urinate into? There's nothing showing, her tight jeans fit smoothly round

11

her skinny hips. She takes a bony hand out of her trouser pocket and picks up a misshapen St. Barbara, with a pin-sized head and an enormous arm and hand raised in the air. With her other hand she starts to move the wooden arm up and down. I sense she can tell she's annoying me with her game and is doing it on purpose as a way of saying that all these objects are utterly worthless. We stay silent for a few moments, while she amuses herself with her little game and I close my eyes as the sea and dunes fade away. I open my eyes again in time to see her doubled up, trying to suppress a twinge of pain, but before I can say anything she's on her feet and, blushing, asks me to excuse her for a minute, she'll be right back. She disappears down the far corridor, and I can hear the door being locked. There's something wrong with her, or is she putting it on? Perhaps she wants to go through the array of perfume bottles crowding the onyx shelf. I feel ashamed of myself. How can my grandparents have played such a dirty trick on me? An onyx shelf is just the sort of thing they'd have dreamed about, though my grand-mother would never have imagined such a thing as perfume existed. She must be sitting on the toilet looking at them and thinking she may admire me but I'm just a bloody bourgeoise. Or maybe she's smiling understandingly. It's even worse when they feel sorry for you; they sympathise and smile benevolently, like the two of them clambering on the wire fence at the airport. They kept shouting after me, 'Mother, your fur coat is trailing on the ground! Mind you don't catch your rings in it!' they kept on shouting and laughing and I stopped and laughed too and for a moment felt like running over to the fence and flinging the fur coat over the top, and the rings after it, so they'd see they didn't really matter to me, but I thought they might be offended so all I did was trail my coat on the ground even more and drag it up the gangway into the plane like a dead animal, while they laughed and clapped and swung on the fence like monkeys and I roared with laughter and the stewardess laughed too. Everyone was laughing except for two male figures sitting right at the front

12

of the plane, who stared at me icily. I did the only decent thing in the circumstances. I stopped in the aisle and, looking them straight in the eye, shook the dust off the coat in their direction. They turned their faces away, livid. And what if one of them, in the street, suddenly recognises the boy swinging on the wire fence, waving and making V-signs? Though all young people look pretty much alike. Even Dolores hasn't changed much. She looks virtually the same at twenty-eight as she did at twenty-three, while in the course of the last five years I've stopped looking young. I say 'looking' because I stopped being young a long time ago, but managed to go on looking it. Otherwise I'd never have tolerated the miniskirt I was wearing the day it all happened. It seems embarrassing in present circumstances to remember a miniskirt but then... No matter how grotesque it seems to associate such terrible things with a miniskirt, it's there, like it or not, standing out like a fetish in the midst of the horror. The image is lodged in my mind, I can't get rid of it; it's the miniskirt rather than myself I see in the middle of the street, when everyone started running for their lives. Perhaps it's because I had nothing to do with what was happening — and what in God's name was happening? — and I'd caught sight of my distant reflection, full-length, in a shop window that extended to the pavement, and had thought how amazing it was that people should walk around in public like that, like a Renaissance pageboy. I was furious that I'd got mixed up in something. It would probably mean the end of that night's performance. I shouldn't have agreed to give it, especially when it was a benefit for something that didn't concern me; but he'd taken the trouble to come all the way to Buenos Aires, had persisted despite my excuses and refusal to see him, and finally got me to capitulate. And then, after our meeting, I regretted having wasted so much of his time. Had it been the particular atmosphere of the apartment in Buenos Aires, or that afternoon on the river which suddenly became a once-and-forever experience, or the fact that I was at a loose end? Whatever the case, it had been one of those afternoons that mark you indelibly, and that you spend the rest of your life vainly trying to repeat. Why was everyone running with that look of terror in their eyes?

I felt an urge to relive that day from start to finish, like a schoolchild re-enacting the founding of the nation. Regardless of whether she comes back and sits down, feeling better. Why don't we reconstruct it together? Of course she'd like to! Isn't that what she's come for? Oh Dolores, it doesn't matter that we spent so little time together. What matters is the intensity of this moment, the world we glimpsed, the fear we shared. And I don't mind telling you my hands are permanently frozen, and I'd like to let you take them in your hands to warm them. Let's go through it step by step, hand in hand, like sisters; let's see if what we remember is fact or fiction. It was in the morning that we met at the entrance to the Faculty building; I went down the icy corridors, it can't have been later than 9 or 10. Or rather, we went down them together, to tell the truth I didn't take much notice of you but took advantage of you to take me to his office, since you'd offered. I was expecting to find a warm, dimly-lit study, lined with books, where we'd take up the conversation begun in the Buenos Aires apartment. I was shivering with cold. It wasn't just the temperature but the wind, which got trapped in the courtyards and raced round the surrounding corridors lined with balustrades. To break the silence, I made some remark about how funny it was to see an old hotel turned into a university. Overhead was an elaborate glass roof, covered with students waving and shouting; a poster of Mao dropped through a broken pane and fluttered round in circles. (You said one could easily imagine a party of elegant guests having tea, looking out at the liners berthed in the nearby port.) I told you it looked like the setting for a 1930s movie, I can't remember which. (You didn't give the name.) We could hear the students' slogans but I wasn't at all interested in the demonstration, I'd seen too many rioting campuses

14

before. All I had room for in my head was the comic spec-
tacle of that dilapidated luxury hotel and the prospect of an
imminent meeting with the theatre director. He must be
younger than most other people. As young as this stiff-limbed
girl who'd latched on to me since the previous night. Besides,
I felt I'd shed years after leaving an ageing, moody husband,
drained by the energy he put into his painting, unsure of his
talent, afraid of what the future might bring. And to clinch
my feeling of euphoria, the rehearsal had gone incredibly
well, he'd been delighted and it was bound to be a success.
We'd agreed to meet in the early evening in a café in the
city centre, to see some mutual friends; then we'd go on to
eat at his mother's, and the recital would start at 11. So what
was I doing coming to see him now? (You suddenly switched to the conversation we'd had the night before, after the
rehearsal, when I told you I went to the university in the mornings, right next to the drama school, and you immediately
said you'd like to look round it and I, of course, offered to
take you wherever you wanted to go.) So she'd been at the
rehearsal? But of course, I clearly remember seeing Dolores'
face and that of a few other students dotted around the empty
auditorium. Then she came up the steps towards me, walking stiffly like a child. I was told she was a good writer, one
of the best. Bound to be a lesbian. That exaggeratedly boyish
look, not to mention the blazer with its pockets sagging from
being stuffed with books and files. And that silent adoration
that shone from her eyes in the stalls, and which continued
to shine from that moment on... When we reached the top
floor, we leaned on the balustrade to watch the demonstration on the roof. The few panes of glass left were rattling
with the din. (You took me by the arm and started to tell
me how Norma Shearer, in a slinky, silver-lamé dress, had
sat under the glass roof, sipping tea and looking out at the
port. As she glided over the red carpet, she paused for a split
second to toss back her platinum-blonde hair, and elegantly
made for a table for two by the window. She hitched up her
gleaming skirt as the waiter stood respectfully behind her,

15

ready to draw up her chair, and extracted from her diamanté handbag an enormous powder-puff with which she proceeded to dust her pearly-white face. Then she touched up the bold outline of her lipstick and struck up a forced, enigmatic smile.) I stayed leaning against the balustrade, smiling, fascinated by that make-believe glasshouse. Someone shouted 'Comrades!' and there was an unexpected hush. I'm not going to tell her that I've just remembered. Dolores grabbed my hand and plunged it with hers into her blazer pocket. Her hand felt warm like that of a child. 'A little girl's hand,' I reassured myself. My reflexes deserted me. Instead of disengaging my hand and making for the corridor where it was assumed we'd find him, I let it rest in her pocket and stood there not making any move. I avoided her eyes. I wanted to attribute the gesture to the dazzling effect my presence had had on her. I was also dimly aware that I'd never been able to resist a plea for love. What was I supposed to do next? She must finally have accepted my hand's passivity, its pathetic helplessness, and lifted it out gently, as if it were an inanimate object. She disappeared down the corridor but I was left mortified by the ambiguity of the situation and by the clumsy way I'd handled it. Apart from which the last thing I wanted was to go down in her esteem. As to be expected, he wasn't in his office, I should have known he wouldn't be there on a day like that. (You didn't seem particularly put out and I thought perhaps you'd like to see round my department; but I don't know what happened as we were going downstairs, I looked round to find you and couldn't see you anywhere.) The students came streaming down the stairway and Dolores announced that something was going to happen that afternoon, at the funeral or afterwards. But I felt frustrated, upset. I'd put on this quite unsuitable miniskirt, all for nothing. He'd no sense of timing. Better to forget all about him and concentrate on that night's performance, since there was nothing for it. I was going round in circles, as usual, and this stupid journey was turning out to be a waste of time. I'd have been better off staying in Buenos Aires. I felt, yet again, that the most trivial incident could plunge me into an entirely uncalled-for, irremediable depression. The girl carried on ahead and joined the ranks of a wild, impassioned group pounding down the stairs. The university building emptied in a trice. As the shouting receded into the distance, it was replaced by the howling of the wind as it blasted its way round the corridors. The building was filled with swirling leaves and leaflets. Paralysed with cold, I went along a kind of metal catwalk. I must be very near the port, colourless and flat in the glassy winter light. As I came out into the street, I saw a ship sail into the harbour. No, it wasn't Norma Shearer's liner; just a common-or-garden freighter, with no lights on and no one on deck. Mechanically, it steered its way into the navigation channel. I discovered that a landscape can be the same white as a blind man's eyes. Milky and unfathomable. I cursed everyone, including myself, so energetically and systematically that the feeling started to trickle back into my numb limbs.

She's obviously combed her hair during her second trip to the bathroom. 'With my comb,' the older woman thinks with disgust. But she realises she no longer wants her to leave. It's the first time for days that she's stopped shivering. She's also stopped feeling a compulsive urge to press her fingers against the left hand corner of her mouth. She'll have to invent another pretext to get her to stay. After all, she's only offered her a coffee. But the girl doesn't want tea and toast. How about some strawberry tart? No, really, she replies with a smile. No cheese either, nothing, she never has much of an appetite. Folding her arms over the bulging waistline and stomach she can no longer conceal, the older woman is about to say something silly, like no point casting pearls before swine, but stops herself in time. She realises jokes are out of place in a city that looks as if it had been abandoned, with its shopwindows half-empty and draped with cobwebs. She wonders, for the umpteenth time, why the girl has come and, above all, why she seems happy to stay. The only likely explanation is that she felt a need to be with someone and having found someone... The woman knows how people tend to confide in her and that makes her feel strong again. Isn't that her most familiar role, the one she plays best? Relaxing, she resolves to give whatever is asked of her. Meanwhile Dolores, sunk in her armchair as if for life, sends the odd affectionate look in her direction. The two of them start talking at the same time, and both fall silent, laughing. The second time, as to be expected, the older woman wins. It's ages since she last had news of Luisa. What's she doing nowadays?

'She's not in Montevideo,' Dolores replies curtly. And goes silent again.

It's hard going with someone so laconic, but she refuses to give up. Besides, it was Luisa who...

'I often think of Luisa, and every time I remember her I have an image of her jumping on the table and tightening the lightbulbs; you probably don't even remember.'

'How could I forget...'

She spoke the words with her eyes fixed on a figure in the carpet, tracing its outline with the toe of her shoe. 'Of course I remember,' she murmurs as if unwilling to pursue the matter.

'There are some things I can't get straight. Was she already in the dining room when we all came in?'

The girl looks up at her warily, as if afraid of falling into a trap, then reluctantly capitulates.

'We never bothered to look for her when we went to her house, there was no need to that time either. We all had our own key, it was like a second home to us. We stayed in the dining room because we could hear people talking in the next room. Luisa came in later, when she put that awful music on.'

'I confess I didn't have a clue what was going on at first, and it made me feel uncomfortable that no one had appeared to welcome us. And later on I was even more thrown because,

18

when she came in and you said it was Luisa, she walked past me with a smile as if it were entirely normal to find me there, even though she'd recognised me, I sensed that, but she just gave me a passing kiss and went to put the record player on full blast so she could drag some reluctant boy off to dance.'

Dolores burst out laughing.

'I bet Tomás didn't have a clue what was going on either. He hardly knew Luisa and anyway he was so shy he could hardly open his mouth. We didn't see him all that often, since he was working with the group from Salto. Just his luck that he should have chosen that night to come to Montevideo, of all nights.'

She'd like to ask what happened to Tomás but feels inhibited; that's the worst thing about coming back to Montevideo: asking about people who are bound to have been killed or tortured or are simply 'missing'. Apart from finding the replies distressing, she can't help having the awful feeling that they're proffered with a certain relish. Relief at still being alive, perhaps; but one doesn't like admitting it. As if reading her thoughts, the girl says: Tomás is in prison. At first we knew where, now we don't. When they decide to lose someone, that's that.

'What do you mean, "lose someone"?'

'It's a manner of speaking. So long as you can't put your finger on the bones, or the ashes, or the lid of a coffin; or until a limb turns up floating in the river, or they toss you a hand . . .'

She brusquely mimed the act of severing a hand with a knife.

The woman shuddered. Was she going to start shaking again? This must be stopped, that's enough, I beg of you.

'I still don't understand how Luisa could leap on to the table so nimbly. Not even if she'd been practising in advance. In a flash she picked up the chair against the wall, jumped on to the table, started to switch the lights on by tightening the bulbs and began to sway her arms slowly from side to side, moving towards us and addressing us in a loud, stilted voice.'

'Were the chairs against the wall?'

'Don't you remember? That was the first thing I noticed when I came into the room. They'd been lined up next to the sofa where you and I sat. The huge table was in the middle of the room and on the other side, between the windows, were the sofas where everyone else was sitting.'

'Flaquita and Néstor on one sofa, Tomás on the other and Enrique on the arm of Tomás's seat.'

She'd spoken in an entirely matter-of-fact way and had said 'Enrique' without any trace of emotion.

It was probably the desire to see Luisa's famous house that had made me go with them. Who knows. Whenever I passed the shuttered houses in the Plaza Zabala I always tried to imagine what they were like inside, dark, plush, crammed with furniture. I was fascinated by the opulence of what I supposed to be the carved mahogany cornices, the mysterious, dust-covered objects in eternally closed display cabinets, the moth-eaten velvet curtains blotting out the light, and the sudden glint of a superb, abandoned cut-glass goblet. I coveted the marvels of an interior whose muted browns and greens had become purely tactile.

'The chairs against the wall,' Dolores mimicked teasingly, as if talking to herself. 'Don't you remember?'

The older woman glared at her. How could they be so unaware of the visual and tactile world, so indifferent to the endless pleasures it could afford? Without the visual and the tactile there would be no such thing as sensuality, and without sensuality there would be no such thing as eroticism. What kind of orgasms did they have in their austere world? She heard herself describing Luisa's apartment inch by inch. She might as well go to town while she was about it. The room was an irregular shape, with the far right wall at an angle. You came straight into the main room, believe it or not. Down the steps from the entrance hall into the main room. The distance between the door and the windows was disproportionately large, which was no doubt why Luisa had broken up the space with the huge table placed across the room, and possibly also why the chairs were lined up against one wall. She was disappointed to find that there was nothing mysterious about the room and, despite the carved furniture, it looked bare, as if adrift. Against the side wall was a display cabinet packed with tiny objects. Above it hung a large painting that looked like a Dutch landscape blackened with age. The houses were much more mysterious when you imagined what they were like from the outside, standing in the shady gardens of the Plaza Zabala. Even the thick, threadbare velvet curtains, which came the closest to matching her expectations, lacked the appropriate aura of clandestinity. She could see the curtains in her mind's eye and laughed out loud, as if she were again standing in front of those wondrous objects.

'I bet you never even saw them. I mean the cats, Dolores... You know, the cats!'

Dolores frowned but then burst into a broad grin.

'The cats! How could I have forgotten the cats! You pointed them out to me gleefully but they stared at us suspiciously from on top of the pelmets, desperately digging in their claws to keep their balance.'

'One of the pelmets was about to come down any minute.'

'Luisa adored her Siamese cats, but we didn't. We used to give them a good kick whenever we got the chance. That's why the poor things used to take refuge on top of the pelmets.'

'Why didn't you like them?'

'They were a present from the Commissioner of Police, that's why.'

Of course she'd no idea. She felt the air pressure drop in the set she'd conjured up. It really was a stage-set, it wasn't her imagination running away with her this time. The set for a real-life drama. With its own tempo and duration. Everyone had played his or her allotted role. She'd forgotten the names of the actors, but now the girl had jogged her memory. Tomás and Enrique sitting facing her, Flaquita and Néstor on the other side of the table. Dolores beside her, chatting to her on the sofa. Not even in dreams could it be

21

replayed differently. The scene was forever attached to an otherwise insipid night, which could have passed off uneventfully like so many others.

And yet everything else that had happened that day had shaded into the mists and vagaries of memory. Less than two days in that city had splintered into so many bits and pieces that it had become impossible to separate the real from the imaginary. Not even with Dolores' help, which was not exactly forthcoming. There was no way she could remember how she'd got to the apartment block, or why she'd bothered to go in the first place after that frustrating afternoon. Or maybe that was precisely why; that or her sudden desperation when the cancellation of that night's performance was confirmed and she realised she wouldn't have another chance to see him. The most sensible thing would have been to return to Buenos Aires that same night. What was there left for her to do in that strife-torn city? But she'd insisted on wandering round the streets, observing the aftermath of the afternoon's disturbances out of the corner of her eye, refusing to call it a day. He'd rung to say he probably wouldn't be able to make it to dinner at his mother's; but that she, of course, was still welcome. The old couple would be delighted to meet her. Such a pity the show had had to be cancelled. Never mind, another time. He didn't sound all that upset. She'd hung up and dialled his mother. Yes, he'd just sent a message to say he might not be able to make it but he couldn't be certain; he'd do his best. And would she still be coming? She said yes. She was so put out by things not going according to plan that she was damned if she wasn't going to see things through to their proper conclusion. Her whole life had been devoted to organising the world around her, and nothing exasperated her more than something refusing to fit in. Hovering out of reach, at the mercy of chance. And so it was, just before nine o'clock, that she found herself in the unlikely situation of taking the lift up to that tiny flat which, yet again, looked out over the port. It was the last thing she wanted to see but, no sooner had she come in the door, than the old couple steered her over to a window like a porthole to admire the view. She peered out apprehensively but was reassured. In the dark, the blind man's eye had turned into a black hole. 'Over there in the distance, can you see it?' the old couple insisted, pointing at the void. Better that way; better than just to carry on floating in that cramped, badly-lit room, drifting in the dark.

They retired to the kitchen adjoining the dining room, to concoct in my honour a soup that defied all description. They kept on tossing things into it, muttering under their breath as if performing some ritual. He, of course, showed no sign of turning up, and I realised the old couple were as sorry they'd invited me as I was that I'd come. As they toiled away in the kitchen, I tried to recall what little I knew about them. His mother had been an active public figure in the field of education; having lost her husband at an early age, she'd devoted her life to bringing up the son who'd eluded me throughout the day. On retirement, she'd undergone a complete change of personality; the tough, forbidding woman she'd been before turned overnight into a dithering old granny, taking refuge in the local cinemas, emerging blinking from the matinées to totter to the Plaza San Martín, where she would carefully get out the bags of crumbs she'd brought for the pigeons. Her friends, concerned at her sudden decline, no longer recognised her. They were even more concerned when, out of the blue, she announced to her nearest and dearest that she was marrying her present husband. They wrote him off completely. He had no job and probably never had had, despite vague references to a theoretical pension that had something to do with customs and excise. He looked younger than she, in his one shiny suit, which he kept polishing with the nails of his thumb and index finger. It had been a park-bench romance. Gossip had it that he'd never done a day's work in his life except for feeding the pigeons, but even then she had to provide him with the crumbs.

23

Contrary to expectation, however, remarriage gave back to his mother something of her former assertiveness. Almost posthumously, the two of them switched roles; she, never having been one to fuss, took on his foibles lock, stock and barrel, turning their life in the apartment block into a daily round of trivia. He, having been something of a gay dog and a shyster, took on the cowed look of a naughty schoolboy caught in the act. Once a month, she would go out on her own to collect her teacher's pension; he, far from taking offence, would count the days eagerly and, as soon as she was out of sight, would go down to the café over the road to have a beer and gamble with his former mates. It was his secret life.

As she watched them stirring the soup in the pan, she thought that the gossip was an understatement. She tried to get some information out of them about what had happened that afternoon, but they didn't even know anything had happened. At the top of their apartment block, they were almost completely cut off from the outside world. 'Do you suppose that's why?' his mother said, leaving the question hanging in the air. The old man came over to chat to her. He told her how the nurse from the hospital still brought him fresh eggs regularly, a year after he'd had his haemorrhoid operation, on the National Health at that. It was a real blessing, because they were five centavos cheaper than in the market. He knew the cheapest places to get everything. He gave a sly smile, as if he'd found a way of bringing down the regime. She started to feel claustrophobic with the portholes and the old man's inane conversation. She asked if she could go to the bathroom and he went with her to indicate that she had to wash her hands with the pink soap shaped like a bear, not the other one, and to hand her the towel which, he pointed out, was strictly for guests. By the time they got back the soup was served, but the old man, out of deference to the distinguished guest, refused to tuck his serviette into his knitted waistcoat. Which gave rise to a protracted argument that started by complaining about the stains on his clothes and unforeseeably degenerated into a violent row in the course of which frequent mention was made of the attendant at a Japanese laundry. She ate her soup valiantly and, as soon as she'd downed the last spoonful, excused herself and got up to go to the phone. There was a dismayed hush but she no longer cared, to hell with them. More fool her for having been so stupid. It was the third time that day she'd found herself in an embarrassing situation because of that bloody man. She reacted, as usual in such cases, by becoming aggressive. Didn't she have the whole night ahead of her? She was thinking of ringing some old friends, but the first number she found was that of Dolores. Anyone would have thought she'd been waiting for her call. Could they come and pick her up? Yes, please, as soon as you can. Yes, of course the show had been cancelled with all the street disturbances. Yes, by all means, whatever you like. Dolores's voice sounded choked with emotion at the other end of the line.

'If you'd had any idea of what was going to happen would you still have come with us?'

'God, I'd have gone anywhere, no matter what I thought was going to happen. I felt like screaming. I didn't even thank the poor old couple for the soup... Remember, I'd been going round in circles like an idiot ever since the morning. And the show being cancelled was the last straw. So many things going wrong in one day was too much.'

The girl gave her a quizzical look, but she didn't notice. At that moment, animated by the conversation, she looked the younger of the two women. She'd spent days in total isolation, buried in despair. Now she was coming back to life with a vengeance.

'Did the riot catch you at the spot where we found you?'

'I can't remeber, let me think. First I went to the theatre, which was closed, and then I crossed the main avenue to turn off down San José, I can't think why.'

She did know why, but didn't want to tell her she was going

25

to meet him in a café. She wasn't sure whether they were good friends or mere acquaintances. But they must know each other quite well, since Dolores and her friends had been at the theatre the night before and had stayed on for the rehearsal. She remembered he'd put his arm round her when he introduced her. A bony, angular girl, with eager eyes, an avid mouth, yet another admirer.

'I realised something was amiss when they started to pull the metal shutters down. The brutes... They all clattered to the ground at once, just imagine, so there was nowhere you could hide, while the wretches stood there peeking out from behind the shutters. Before you knew what had happened, the street had turned into a gigantic trap; not a single café or shop or doorway open. In a split second.'

Dolores was smiling to herself.

'I was amazed you could run so fast with those high heels.'

She's going to say 'and with that miniskirt' she thought with a wince; but Dolores went no further. Come to that, she and Flaquita had been wearing miniskirts too, though nothing quite like hers.

'Bloody shoes! But right then I swear I didn't even notice them. The only thing in my head was the need to run as fast as I could to escape the cloud of gas that was getting thicker and thicker. It's just as well I'd had plenty of practice at running for it in the street, and in Buenos Aires it was always worse, with the horses on top of you. What I hadn't anticipated was that the army had everything planned, so when I got to the crossing out of breath and saw them coming from both sides, I panicked.'

'You'd forgotten you were in a rational, civilised country.'

'Yes, I didn't have time to think about things like that. If they were coming from behind and from the streets on either side, the only option was to keep on running. You didn't have to be a genius at logistics to work that one out. But what I couldn't fathom was why I couldn't see anyone running ahead of me. I still can't understand it. Why wasn't there anyone ahead?'

'But there was! The whole of our group was a couple of blocks further up the avenue. But no one was risking making a run for it on their own. The thing was to beat the columns advancing from both sides and get to the square before them. Once you're in the square it's hard for them to get you, there are too many escape routes.'

'Did I see you first, or did you waylay me?'

'I waylaid you because you looked as if you were running blindly in any direction and were heading straight for them. And by that time they were out for the kill, after all that had happened. It was no joke. I ran out and dragged you into the middle of our group. That was when we saw them coming from the square as well. Shit! Trapped on all sides. The only way out was the theatre.'

My mohair coat weighs me down like a ton of bricks. I can hear someone calling my name, it must be a mistake. Then I catch sight of the pointed face and greasy hair of the girl at the rehearsal. She's in the middle of a group of people who look relatively calm. I watch her run towards me and grab me by the arm. I can't make out what she's saying and I don't care, I let her take me in tow and they push me into a building I hadn't even noticed was there. They shove me through a half-open door and then down a long corridor. Are we going downhill or is it my imagination? I can dimly hear the unmistakable sound outside of a tear gas canister exploding. Then a series of shorter, sharper reports; machine guns? rifles? (The students were yelling 'Watch out, gunfire' and flinging themselves flat on the floor.) I feel dizzy in this cavity brimming with adolescence. (And a little girl of about fifteen who looks more like twelve screaming hysterically, 'Shoot if you like but don't set the horses on us, don't set the horses on us.') The group makes its way to the end of the corridor, goes up some steps, draws back a bolt, goes through a space and closes behind it what looks like a stagedoor. When my eyes get used to the yellow lighting I realise we really are on a stage.

'The Tapia Theatre saved our lives more than once. Especially after it was gutted by fire, or they set fire to it, who knows. But then the police worked out what was going on and placed a military guard on both exits. So we couldn't use it any more. Anyway, by then it would have been pointless. With the turn events took later on, it would have been naive to take refuge in a theatre. That day we were still playing at cops and robbers. A childish, innocent game to liven things up a bit in the "Switzerland of South America", as they used to call it.'

'From hide-and-seek to the holocaust,' the older woman remarked. 'It's beyond belief.'

She regretted the words as soon as they'd left her lips. How could she indulge in pretty phrases when talking to someone who'd lost everything? She tried to make amends.

'It didn't strike me as at all odd that we should end up on stage, you know. All I felt was a desperate desire to take my shoes off and warm my feet by a little heater someone had switched on. I was totally oblivious to what was going on. I have to confess I wasn't the slightest bit interested in what you were muttering, either. It was like a sketch I was watching for the umpteenth time.'

The girl went red.

'That was an exceptional day. I can assure you it wasn't the first time we'd had to run from the military or they'd used their batons on us. But that day was different. Probably because it was the first time we'd had a student martyr; it makes me blush now to think that we organised the funeral with more rejoicing than sorrow. It wasn't just the novelty of the situation, I hasten to add, but the fact that it made us feel that now we had a reason to start fighting in earnest.'

'And they retaliated in earnest. Do you know what sticks most in my mind? The image of someone up on stage saying: "We won't let them have a second corpse." '

'It sounds like a joke,' Dolores said after a pause. And smiled.

I wouldn't have said it sounded like a joke. Not even at the time. On the contrary, I found it very moving that someone should have taken a decision like that. I forgot all my exhaustion and aching feet. A decision has to be respected. What I'd like to know is: at what point did people start to falter. At what point did two deaths stop sounding a lot, at what point did a hundred deaths stop sounding like a blood-bath? That's what disturbs me. Because once that point has been reached, the frontier between life and death no longer exists. The two things simply become interchangeable, identical. And that's something I can't condone. Because the day I resign myself to the fact that death has ceased to be a matter for protest, I shall have accepted — now that hundreds of people have been killed and you can no longer tell who's dead and who's alive — that it makes no difference that nothing will be left of me when I die; just a carcass, an empty shell. Has Dolores thought of that? Or has she stopped fighting the idea that death is the end of everything? Does she no longer identify life with happiness and death with the most intolerable, appalling grief? Is that what enables her to mention Enrique's name so coolly? What change has taken place in her that I can't fathom, having spent the last few nights agonising at the thought that something dreadful — I can't bring myself to say or even think the word — may have happened to them in Santiago?

But if that were the case, if Dolores belonged to some hitherto unknown human species, there was no need for her to measure her words so carefully. She decided to tackle things head-on.

'The people who took refuge in the theatre, were they the same people who came to fetch me that night in the Volkswagen? Can you clarify that for me? Later that night I recognised a big fellow who looked like a football champion.'

'Tomás. We were talking about him just now, remember? They beat him till his spine broke in two, but that was before they moved him and we lost track of him. I've already told you we don't know what's become of him. The last few times we were able to visit him, he was in a wheelchair.'

'How awful!' she gasped.

'There's no need to feel like that about it. Worse things have happened to other people. Tomás' morale was unshakeable. We used to take him the books he asked for, because, if he wasn't going to be able to go on fighting actively for the cause when he came out, he at least wanted to finish his studies. But it seems the bastards kept taking his books away from him and tearing them to shreds in front of him. It's odd, but I think that upset him more than having been left a cripple for life.'

She felt a lump in her throat. 'I can't understand it,' she murmured finally.

'No, it's hard.'

Her voice betrayed no emotion. She lit up a cigarette.

'And do you remember Enrique? My husband? He was almost closer to Tomás than to me, they spent all their time together. Fortunately Tomás never found out what happened to Enrique. Unless they were cruel enough to show him his body before they threw it into the coffin. They're notorious for doing things like that.'

They both fell silent. The woman was struggling to control her emotions. She would have hated herself if her voice had quivered or faltered.

'Imagining things is worse,' she finally came out.

'I'm not so sure. If you imagine all manner of things, the worst, the most unlikely, the most monstrous thing you can think of, you're only limbering up for reality. I think things are bearable only when you've been able to imagine something worse.'

But the woman said nothing in reply, and now it was the girl's turn to try to steer the conversation back on a steady course.

'Enrique grew a moustache because he looked a little boy, too young for his responsibilities. It was funny watching him twiddling his moustache all day long . . .'

The woman buried her head in her hands and leant forward till it touched her knees.

'You can't have taken it so calmly. I don't believe it, I don't believe it.'

Had Dolores's voice gone quieter or had she decided to block it out? She had to get out of this nightmare, the only way was to go back to the image of herself leaning against the peeling wall of the stage, having got her breath back and warmed her bare feet, listening to the rhythmic flow of the dialogue. She felt a sudden rush of love for those muffled voices, like shuttles plying their way back and forth, far from the sound of the tear gas canisters exploding. She was just beginning to feel at ease when, behind them, they heard a door slam. After a silence, the boy with the moustache ordered some of them to leave and others to stay. Dolores helped her on with her shoes and dragged her off again. The boy with the moustache stayed behind, after patting Dolores on the cheek. He had a fragile look about him, as if better suited to playing the violin or writing poetry than to giving orders, but no doubt his charisma stemmed from the contrast between his firmness and his fragility. She would have liked him to come with them. She had the impression he was the only one who knew what they were doing, while the others were going through the motions. Without a word, Dolores pushed her down the gangway into the orchestra pit. They made their way through the empty stalls, coming out into a foyer that was completely black. No one spoke. 'Isn't it dangerous to go out of the front entrance?' she whispered in the girl's ear. 'No, the theatre is closed because there was a fire.' She began to get used to the dark. She could make out a marble figure holding a singed lamp. Its charred arms made it look grotesque. She began to realise what a stupid situation she'd got herself into. The show was bound to be cancelled and there was nothing to justify her presence in the city. She told Dolores her hotel was two or three blocks away and, since the danger was over, the best thing was for her to go straight back to her room and stay there till the next morning, when she'd leave first thing for Buenos Aires. Or perhaps even tonight. She noticed the look of disappointment in the girl's eyes. Why could she never resist? She took a card out of her bag and held it out so she could jot down the phone number where she could be contacted that evening. If she was still here, she might give her a ring. What were they thinking of doing? Nothing much, the girl answered, we'll probably go to Luisa's, it depends. If we do, she'd love to meet you, the two of you are very alike. Luisa who?, she asked, but the girl was so excited at the prospect she didn't even hear. The whole group will be there, you'll be among friends, they all think you're wonderful; my husband, Flaquita and Néstor, Tomás, Juan.

She tried to remember their names as she waited in the doorway, frozen. The old couple had bade her an icy farewell, too bad. They'd be eating the leftover soup for days to come. The Volkswagen screeched to a halt outside, after turning the corner like a racing car. Dolores went through their names again. This is Tomás, you've already met my husband Enrique, this is Néstor and Flaquita, the one at the wheel is Juan. They all muttered something, except for Juan who carried on hurtling through the empty streets like a madman. Dolores whispered to her that the car had to be handed over by eleven, adding that they had to take such a roundabout route to avoid passing a police station. The word she used wasn't 'police station', but she deduced that was what she meant. The conversation proceeded in fits and starts, almost drowned by the screeching of the Volkswagen. The two boys leaned forwards to make more room for the two women, but even so she could feel Dolores's bony body jammed into hers. Every now and then Enrique would look round and smile at her. She felt more and more comforted by his presence. She thought that, if she were Dolores, she'd spend all her time staring at him and worshipping him instead of wasting her time with all those silly meetings. The girl nicknamed Flaquita turned round twice but when their eyes met she turned away immediately. No one would have said she was more than twelve. She was sitting on her boyfriend's knees. In between the two of them and the one driving lay a guitar. She stared at it, unable to suppress a feeling of disgust. She bitterly regretted having made that idiotic call. What did they have in common? Now she'd have to sit through some ghastly singsong and there'd be no way of getting back to the hotel unless someone took pity on her. She asked Dolores if it was a long way but she assured her it wasn't, it was just that they had to go round in circles to avoid the . . . and she said the word again. She sighed and looked out of the window. Never had she seen the streets so deserted. Not a single soldier or police car or taxi or passerby. It looked like the beginning of the end of the world. Clouds of leaflets left from the afternoon's demonstration swirled to and fro in the gusts of wind blowing from the river. Crumpled sheets of newspaper and posters torn to shreds swished their way along the pavements and piled up on the streetcorners.

They came out into a square. The Volkswagen pulled up by the kerb. As she got out she noticed they were outside some gardens fenced off by a low railing. Something made her look at the houses and she instantly recognised where they were. She couldn't believe it; they were so near the old couple's apartment that, if she'd come on foot, she'd only have had to walk a few blocks through the old part of town and cross the main square. They went into the gardens and stopped under a bushy tree, as the car shot off and Flaquita, after exchanging a few words with the others, marched across the road, heading for the far corner. She came straight back and signalled them that all was clear. They crossed over to the corner and went into a house. They stopped in the freezing hallway while someone lit a cigarette lighter and they proceeded up the staircase. The draughts whistled round the stairwell. They tiptoed their way up. In the flicker of the cigarette lighter she could make out the white marble banisters on every step. To think she'd spend the whole day shivering with cold, in a state of fruitless expectancy, as if to prove the futility of the vast majority of her acts. But suddenly the light fell on a carpeted step, then another and yet another, her feet trod on a pattern made up of arabesques and faded flowers, and a familiar warmth invaded her. 'We're almost there,' the girl whispered at her side. She felt like amusing herself at her expense. She took hold of her hand, as delicately as the girl had done that morning in the university, and clasped it to her bosom; her heart was beating wildly after the steep climb. They looked into each other's eyes and the woman flashed an irresistible smile at her; she was starting to feel better and to view life as a great adventure. Anyone who wanted to join her on it had only to follow her lead.

I couldn't understand why no one came to the door to let us in, but instead Flaquita inserted the key into the lock and walked in as if she owned the place; neither could I understand why we stayed in that dining room that looked like a furniture warehouse, when voices and laughter could be heard in the next room. But I gave in to exhaustion and sensuous delight, sinking into the feather cushion on the velvet sofa next to a row of carved wooden chairs. I beckoned to Dolores to come and sit beside me. Immediately I spotted the Siamese cats, crouching absurdly on top of the pelmets, keeping a wide-eyed watch on us. Not even they could make me stir from that seat, which I felt I'd earned after such a disastrous day. Everything acquired a velvet texture as my senses began to take over. There was a damp patch on the dark beige curtains, just under the pelmet that was threatening to come down. The sparkle of a wine glass cut with a set of initials, in the drinks cabinet at the far end of the room, danced before my eyes. I stretched out my hand to stroke the lush tassles of the runner covering the table. The exquisite upholstery of the sofa on the other side of the room enveloped me in a silken caress. So everything was in its proper place. Even the sounds coming from the next room could be classified according to pitch. A contralto voice seemed to be calling the tune. Luisa? There were occasional ripples of laughter.

Male voices — possibly elderly — and less distinct female replies. I felt ready to share such epiphanies with the young writer. I noticed she was also starting to relax. She'd flopped onto the ample cushions and was resting her head on the curved wooden back. I left her to her thoughts. On reflection, the huge dining room had the look of an elegant brothel, mainly because of the glow of the chandelier hanging high above the table. The little candle-shaped lights were capped with mauve satin shades, and less than half of them were lit. Presumably the owner of the house had loosened them to save electricity. At that moment there appeared in the doorway leading to the next room the figure of Norma Shearer who should have been having tea in the glasshouse where the students had been chanting their slogans. I was disappointed to see that her satin tunic was black and not silver, but the diamanté shoulder-straps made up for it. They matched a tiny bag she was clutching in her hand. She directed an all-embracing nod at the new arrivals, with an impeccable cover-girl smile, then came towards me and gave me a quick peck on the cheek. 'Luisa,' the girl managed to stammer, 'I've brought. . .' but Luisa was already making a beeline for the far end of the room, brushing against the tassels of the table-runner as if her movements were programmed and took precedence over all else. When she got to the other end of the room, she raised the lid of a stereo set, next to the drinks cabinet, and put on a record at such a volume that we were left stunned. Flaquita made a move to get up and say something to her, but she swept her aside and gracefully invited her boyfriend to dance. I expected him to protest, but to my surprise he meekly allowed himself to be carried off to the empty space between the table and the windows. Everyone else looked on, in silence. As she passed the seat where Enrique and the athletic young man were sitting, she smilingly disengaged herself from her companion, leaning her head back like an actress in a silent movie, and disappeared back into the next room. The boy dithered for a second, went over to the sofa where his girlfriend had been left sitting and invited her to dance. Flaquita wound both arms around his neck and they danced cheek to cheek. Norma Shearer came back almost immediately, but this time dragging in her wake a man who presumably was one of the people in the other room. In dismay, I began to think that the night had an unending supply of surprises in store for me. Now two separate dance floors had been created, one on either side of the huge oval table. Hadn't it occurred to anyone to move it to one side?

I turned towards Dolores; to my surprise, her face was again tense and alert. Her lank hair fell over her shoulders in untidy strands. Would she be offended if I pulled out the hair inside her shirt collar? I tried to make up for having ignored her and started to ply her with questions: what did she do? What sort of things did she write? Was she a student? How long had she been married to Enrique? She replied obediently and as she spoke her face started to relax again. They had to live at his parents' house, because both she and Enrique were still students. She was halfway through her teacher's training course, Enrique had almost finished. It was a nuisance, because his parents could only give them a room barely big enough for a bed. They'd fixed up a plank to take the books but it was really an awful mess.

'Enrique's mother gets cross because she says she can't ever clean the place properly with so many bits of paper lying around and the house will get full of cockroaches.'

'Why don't you hang some shelves on the wall?'

'We tried but the wall isn't strong enough, that's the trouble. The shelf we put up has fallen down twice, bringing the plaster with it. It's just as well it happened during the day.'

'Your mother-in-law must have been furious.'

'She never found out, we covered the hole up before she saw it. We pinned a poster over it.'

'And how long is it before Enrique graduates?'

'God knows. They keep closing the university all the time. Up till last year things weren't too bad. But this year...'
She stopped to correct herself. 'Well, now things are going

36

better, but from a different point of view.'

'I suppose you're pregnant?'

The girl went bright red and gave the woman a somewhat hostile look.

'And why do you suppose that?'

'Because all the revolutionaries I've ever met keep producing babies.'

'So what? We probably think we haven't got much time.'

'She might as well have said one has to produce a new generation of fighters,' she thought wearily. It was clear that life with this girl would not exactly be a bowl of cherries. Why were they all so dreary, so humourless, so flat? She wondered whether tiny things ever made her happy. Did she appreciate what it was to wake up in the morning and see a tree, for example? Young people didn't know how to use their eyes, no one had ever taught them, and without that faculty they were bound to get things wrong. Was that why they flung themselves into action as if flinging themselves under a train? You have to find some way of living life to the full, and she had to admit their method had the merit of being original. Conversation was replaced by action; individual pleasure by group discipline. 'They're going to have a hell of a time,' she thought; 'they do what they want in the same way we used to say what we wanted. But doing is more dangerous than talking.' She couldn't really understand why she liked their company more than that of her own generation. What did they have that attracted her? They were ignorant, inflexible, austere, they didn't believe in culture or beauty; what could be worse? And what was Luisa doing mixing with them? She guessed she must be about the same age as herself. She remembered Dolores had suggested in passing that they were alike. And what did they have in common? Their need to seduce an audience. She was suddenly made aware of the fragility and pettiness of this stylish display of seductive charms. 'Whores; that's what we are when it comes to it, whores.' Once again she was assailed by the depression that had dogged her throughout the day. There was something false in all this and she had to find out what. What was Dolores saying? She stopped listening to her boring conversation. She didn't care a damn about the banalities of her life. The baby would soon be born and would be put in a cot in the kitchen or the bathroom because there was no room anywhere else. Her mother-in-law would look after it, begrudgingly, while she went off to her clandestine meetings. And her mother-in-law would be right; what right had they to spoil other people's lives by producing children, when they weren't even prepared to take care of them? Times had changed, indeed; she'd spent three years of her life barely going out of the house watching over her newborn son, listening to him breathe at night, leading him by the hand, showing him the world. Now everything had changed, but there was little cause for celebration.

To think that she'd landed in the middle of an impromptu party in a flat in old Montevideo, of all things. They could have chosen a better day... But they seemed to be having a great time. Flaquita and her partner were still dancing ecstatically, his hands buried in her thick mane of hair, which was the only sensuous thing about her. The owner of the house was trying out various dance steps with the man from the other room who, bemused but stiff, let her take the lead. Another man, tall and thin, with white hair, appeared in the doorway and Luisa's partner muttered something in her ear and disengaged himself gently. Luisa invited the tall man to dance. The other man looked on, leaning against the doorframe. He seemed to be engrossed in inhaling his cigarette. Somewhere a telephone rang and the man turned on his heels and disappeared, as if expecting the call. I saw Luisa stop dancing, run over to the boy with the sportman's physique and whisper something in his ear. She was standing with her back to me. She must be getting on in years, but she carried herself with a slightly old-fashioned elegance and stateliness that matched the heavy curtains and carved furniture. Was she single, married, divorced? Probably divorced; she had that confidence that comes from regaining one's freedom at a time of life when one had thought it lost for ever. The man reappeared framed in the doorway and only then did I notice his incredible aura of authority. Clearly someone used to giving orders. The slight sneer on his tightly pressed lips gave his face a cruel look. It was at that point that events took such an incredible turn, as Luisa pulled the chair up to the table, leapt on to the burgundy velvet runner, looked up at the chandelier hanging high above her head, swiftly raised both arms, and started to twist the tiny bulbs that lit up one by one as if by magic. A steely light flooded the room. Standing on the table, Luisa looked taller than she was. The unflattering glare showed up the bulging contours of her waist and stomach. She was declaiming in the most absurd fashion, the disjointed words rang out like whiplashes, quite out of context, her eyes were half-closed and she was gesticulating melodramatically. It was a few seconds before it dawned on me that she was reciting something, who'd have thought it! Someone had lifted the needle off the record and the moment of truth had come. She strode from one end of the table to the other as she went on with the recital, for that's what it was, though her movements were measured and calculated. I looked at the others. They were watching her transfixed, their faces absolutely straight. I looked at the man standing in the doorway to the other room and a shiver ran down my spine. In the light, the contours of his skull stood out beneath the skin. Suddenly Luisa's advance along the red velvet runner was interrupted by the sound of a key turning in the front door, the door opened, in came Juan, the driver of the Volkswagen, his fists clenched and his arms pressed against his sides, he blinked with the glare, looked up at the table and recoiled in amazement, then looked at Enrique with what seemed to be a slight shrug of the shoulders and Luisa stopped dead in her tracks, turning to look down at him from on high. She too lowered both arms and let them hang stiffly, left stranded and utterly ridiculous in her exposed position till the man in the doorway made a move, advanced into the centre of the room, slid the chair to the end of the table so she could get down and offered her his hand, muttering something inaudible. But she left his hand dangling in mid-air, found another chair and leapt nimbly to the floor, saying clearly: 'Let's get this straight, no one bursts into my parties without my permission.' The man lowered his arm and, evidently put out, straightened his jacket. His voice was quivering with rage as he replied: 'And no one kills my men without my permission, either,' in a loud voice for everyone to hear. It was then that I realised the boy who'd come in was not alone; several men in uniform were standing behind him.

'As the Commissioner of Police wishes,' Luisa was heard to say. 'I give my assurance there won't be any trouble.' She looked at the young people one by one. She came over to my side and sat on the arm of the sofa, but got up straightaway to shake hands with the boy who'd just come in. He was white as a sheet. 'I'm sure it can all be explained,' Luisa said, 'there's always some maniac who takes advantage of the unrest to stir up trouble.' 'Outside all of you, on the double,' a sinister fellow growled, standing in front of me. 'All of us?' I asked. In fact the question was not directed to anyone in particular, but the Commissioner of Police felt obliged to be precise. 'Everyone who was in the Volkswagen that was stopped.' 'But,' Luisa started to say. Dolores, on her feet, held out her hand to me and murmured, 'It's best to do as they say, in your case things will be cleared up in no time at all.' I don't know why I made no attempt to resist but went out into the freezing entrance hall as if in a dream. I turned and caught a glimpse of the Commissioner of Police picking up the diamanté bag that Luisa had dropped when she got up on the table, and handing it to her. But Luisa stood rigid watching us go out of the door, ignoring his existence. I got the impression he was blushing. In the hallway three grim men, leaning against the wall, leapt to attention when the Commissioner of Police appeared. Luisa came as far as the door, pressing both arms stiffly against her black satin gown. Any resemblance to Norma Shearer had vanished.

40

'I'd like to see her again. When all this is over, or I get some news . . .'

'It's too late, she left a couple of months ago. She sold off most of her belongings and locked up the apartment, like everyone else. To be fair, she did what she could over the last few years, but she was on their blacklist after that. She went to France to stay with a sister who's lived in Lyons for years. I can't imagine them getting on, Luisa was too used to doing what she liked, and I gather her sister is an old fusspot who thinks she's crazy. Anyway, what was there to keep her here? The romance had gone out of it all. Did you know they interrupt the television programs every night to broadcast the latest update on the military situation, and show photographs of the enemies of the people who've been killed or who are wanted? Full-face, in profile, and with a number underneath; they don't look like human beings. Dangerous delinquents all of them, long-haired or close-cropped, eyes staring, tight-lipped; when my photo was flashed up on the screen, my parents didn't recognise me. And even with this rogues' gallery it's impossible to believe there are so many enemies of the people and that they're fifteen or seventeen years old and toting their machine guns like gangsters; and all of a sudden they flash up the panic-stricken face of a plumber, a dentist, a housewife, you name it, whoever they found listed in some prisoner's address book. There's no rhyme nor reason to it.'

She had to go on.

'Why do you think people no longer look you in the face when they meet you in the street? If a friend sees you getting on the bus he hides behind his newspaper as if you were the devil incarnate, and gets out at the next stop in case you say "Hi!" and it costs him his life.'

Was she exaggerating, like so many of them? Trotting out the same old stories, like clockwork? The outside world of war, earthquakes, changes of government, trips to the moon or Mars or whatever had ceased to exist for them. And having always refused to climb aboard their pathetic life raft, was

I now claiming a place on it too? Dolores droned on mechanically about how she'd got off lightly because at least they hadn't tortured her but had only made her have a miscarriage by stamping on her belly. So that doesn't count as torture? Are you living in cloud-cuckoo-land or something? They just overdid it a bit, the brutes. Torture is an entirely different matter, don't kid yourself. She launched into a classification of types of torture as if reeling off a list of plant species. A few years ago such a conversation would have been unthinkable. I don't understand it, for some time now everything in this place has ceased to be what it was. Now we can talk over a cigarette or a coffee about how someone was made to eat his excrement or drink his urine; no one bats an eyelid, no one thinks of screaming or throwing himself out of the window. These things happen, Dolores went on, all that matters is to survive and, when it happens to you, it changes you. It's hard to describe, it's as if they'd destroyed you for life but at the same time made you immune from death. That must be the case if, after being forced to lie on her back, naked, in the sixth month of pregnancy, while they stamped on her till she lost consciousness, she regards herself as lucky because she's here now talking to me about the awful things that happened to other people. The girl went over to the window and looked out. When she turned around, her wandering gaze was fired with a new intensity. She told me after they'd released her, she'd worked herself into the ground, she didn't say at what. Not having a television set, she didn't see her husband's photo flash up on the screen, with a number underneath, killed in action, when in reality he'd been rotting in prison for over two years. I tried unsuccessfully to visualise Enrique's fragile face on the TV screen. Had they cropped his hair? Shaved off his moustache? I felt ashamed of myself for thinking of such things. She stopped talking, a painful grimace on her wide, avid mouth. She was probably just a girl in need of affection, like any other. Had she come to demand it, with that bitter, cynical tone? Excuse me a minute, she said, and crossed the floor to go to the bathroom again.

No sooner have we got ourselves out of one minefield than we land in another. It's not so much a conversation as an excavation. If only I knew what we're trying to unearth. But she doesn't know the answer to that, nor do I. When she comes back she'll ask me to tell her what happened that night when they separated us in that freezing police station. And suddenly I realise all I can tell her are trivial details. I'll never forget; I can see myself standing, livid with rage, in the middle of that dingy office, while they were spirited off down the far corridor. But why should she care what happened to me? We didn't exchange glances in the police van, when they drove us off. We didn't even say goodbye later on. I didn't even turn my head to look as they bundled them out of the door; my pride wouldn't let me, I couldn't bear the thought of that dirty little creep behind his desk having the power to make me stand in front of him without addressing a word to me.

'I felt guilty that night, you know,' the girl said as she appeared in the doorway. 'We shouldn't have gone to pick you up at the apartment block, because we knew they'd been trailing us for several days. Especially after so many people getting killed that afternoon. But we thought we had the perfect alibi, with Luisa and all that. One never learns.'

'Thinking about it now, I still don't really know what happened.'

'It's not worth thinking about now.'

'They'd rather die than talk,' the woman thought apprehensively. What would her son say when faced with a team of torturers? She must find something else to think about quickly; anything but that, anything but that. She turned back to the image of herself standing in front of the man, pretending to go through her bag. It made no difference, because the man was shuffling his papers as if no one was there. The only two chairs in the room were taken up by two uniformed soldiers, their legs spreadeagled. One was dozing and the other was cleaning his nails with a penknife.

'You were so furious you didn't even look at me when I touched your arm before they carted us off to the cells.'

Had she touched her on the arm? She hadn't even noticed. She stared at the map of Uruguay dotted with fly droppings. Or were they towns? She went on staring at it till she regained her composure. She'd make that swine behind the desk pay for this. She'd mobilise all the contacts she had in high places to denounce him, wreck his career, wipe him off the face of the earth. As if reading her thoughts, the swine snatched her passport from her and started to leaf through it insolently. He moistened each page with saliva as he turned it, and she thought she'd never be able to rid the passport of the smell of stale beer. 'Where do you live?' he asked brusquely. 'In Lima, Peru,' she replied, her confidence returning. 'Argentinian and you live in Lima . . .' the man growled. Then, in a conciliatory tone, she tried to explain that her husband was Peruvian and she'd lived for years in . . . She was cut short by a violent shriek. It took her a few seconds to realise that the shriek was addressed to her and that the inspector was shouting what the hell did he care, the last thing he needed was for foreign enemies of the people to come and tell him what was what.

At that point I realised I'd got things completely wrong. Something had changed radically and I was starting to notice. No matter who I might be, I simply didn't exist for them. Or rather: they decreed who could exist and who could not. And who were they? The scum of the earth, the bottom of the heap; we'd never noticed them till now but they must always have been there in our midst, waiting for the day they could exact their revenge. My fury started to ebb away, and was replaced by a growing puzzlement and curiosity. When I asked, in a calm tone, for permission to speak to the Peruvian Ambassador, I think I expected him to reply. He opened his mouth wide and spat out syllables: 'You can tell the Ambassador to get stuffed.' And after those words I felt things begin to rearrange themselves according to a new logic. I started to look him up and down in fascination. He didn't know what to do with me and was afraid of putting his foot in it. It was quite likely he'd recognised me; besides, there'd been photos in the papers that day, on account of the show that was to have taken place. He got up stretching himself and yawning ostentatiously, but I'd got the initiative back. I knew he was yawning to gain time and he knew I knew. He went over to one of the men sitting down and viciously kicked his boot. The man leapt up and stood to attention awkwardly. 'Get this slut out of here,' he barked without so much as looking at me. 'Put her on the boat that leaves at midnight and hand her over to the appropriate authorities.' I was dumbfounded. Had he won after all? I stammered that I had to fetch my suitcase from the hotel and would he please give me back my passport. He didn't even deign to reply. He tossed the passport to his subordinate, who caught it in mid-air. 'Take her to pick up her luggage and put her on the boat.' The man had my passport and I had no option but to follow him. Game, set and match to the inspector. But the swine had not yet finished. As we were going out of the door, he growled: 'As if we didn't have enough on our hands cleaning up the garbage in our own country.' That was too much. I heard myself shriek like a maniac, turning to confront him head on: 'What garbage do you think you're talking about? Why don't you look at me? Can't you see I'm talking to you?' The two police officers ran over to the desk. But the inspector had been caught off his guard and had finally raised his head. At last I existed, at last he'd looked at me. I was as real as the map of Uruguay, the desk, the chairs. Suddenly weary, I fell silent, but went on looking at him straight in the eye. His eyes were set disproportionately far apart, and were sunk pitifully in his podgy flesh. They had to be like that, either too far apart or else too close together. I decided it was time to bring the scene to a close. I turned on my heels and the police officer ran after me. I imagined that the inspector was still looking at me and would take a while to recover. I felt a gratifying tingle flow through my limbs.

What's the point of telling her all this? Nothing but trivial details that are of no importance to anyone, and that have remained ingrained in the memory out of wounded pride. While perhaps her son... And what does it matter to Dolores that the cold she felt as she left the police station was a different kind of cold, how can she explain, it wasn't just the gale-force wind blowing from the river, or the humiliation when they got to the hotel, with everyone looking at her; this was an internal, organic cold, that stemmed from being at the mercy of something or someone you can't pin down; something that was beginning to take shape, threatening her when she'd thought herself free and immune, how wrong she'd been! Reluctantly, no longer confident she can live up to her reputation as a raconteur, she gives way to Dolores' insistence and tells how the ferry stank of urine and vomit and how it was not exactly an unforgettable night, though in a sense it was, which is why she has no difficulty recalling how she stayed huddled in the couchette, her stomach churning with the tossing of the boat in the choppy waters, and how the cook and the police officer kept coming in and out, and how someone kept popping his head round the door and then disappearing, and the sound of people muttering that went on for hours and hours; the mutterings, the creaking noises, the disgusting smells. The sensation that nothing exists except for one's sensations; one's senses on the alert, mistrustful, expecting the worst; but not a single idea or thought. Her head a complete blank. Is that what happens to you?

'Yes, sometimes. What time did you get to Buenos Aires?'

'At dawn, I suppose, because it was light. When the wretched boat came to a standstill I plucked up courage to smile at the police officer and ask him to give me back my passport.'

'That was pretty naive of you!'

' "Give you back what?" he snapped. "My passport,"
I repeated, trying not to look alarmed. "The inspector will
give it back to you," he said after a pause, "at police headquarters." So the ultimate humiliation consisted in there being
no end to it. I'd thought it was the end of the matter and now
it was starting all over again. And to make things worse,
the longer it went on, the less I felt able to rebel or take a
stand.'

'That happens too.'

'Despite the fact that I kept on telling myself this couldn't
happen to me, it wasn't possible, as the police van raced round
the streets of Buenos Aires till it got to the dreaded Calle
Moreno. It couldn't be true that I had to go into another office
just like the last one, and find myself faced by the same
inspector behind the same desk, and stare this time at the
map of the Argentine Republic. But it was true; standing in
front of the desk I stared grimly at the Bay of Samborombón,
unable to get out of my head the memory of how difficult
I'd found it to draw as a child. Can you imagine! Riveted
by a silly memory, as if transfixed by it . . .'

'It's the only defence one has,' Dolores interrupted. (She
had good reason to know.)

'But the inspector refused to play the game and instead
of saying the Peruvian Ambassador could get stuffed, said
he didn't even know where Peru was (sniggers from his
subordinates), and what the hell did he have to do with Peru,
this is Argentina, sit down and wait.'

Three chairs lined up against the wall: two were occupied
by a little girl like Flaquita in Montevideo, and her boyfriend.
They were holding hands. The boy was pale and the girl was
glowering. She imagined that, when threatened, the girl
would attack but when it came to the crunch he would have
to protect her. She wondered why they were there, looking
lost, as if they ought to be at school. Maybe the classic picture of Argentina as the land of *gauchos* tamed by successive
generations of generals on horseback was not true either.
Maybe something was in the process of change. Whatever

47

the case, the inspector didn't give a damn where Peru was, which would have been unthinkable a few years before. She looked at his thickset neck and the tangle of hair sprouting above his eyes. Things did not look promising. Yet again, the leaves of her passport were moistened by the new inspector's saliva. 'It's got nothing to do with me,' he said after a while. 'You'll have to see the other inspector.' Her voice was wobbling as she asked why. 'Why, why,' the inspector mimicked, clicking his tongue against the roof of his mouth. 'You people always say you don't know why. Because the Uruguayan police have filed a charge against you, that's why, madam. In case you didn't know.' What charge? How was he supposed to know? Had he been responsible for bringing her back from Montevideo? She finally managed to assert herself: What inspector did she have to see? Where? When? Which provoked him into asserting himself in turn; he started to scream hysterically, who did she think she was, she could forget about her passport if that's what she felt like, to hell with Peru, we've got enough garbage here. At first she was thrown, then she appealed silently to the young couple for help. 'I'd make sure you get your passport back if I were you,' the girl reflected. 'Once you've lost it you'll never get another one.' 'Shut up!' the new inspector thundered. Now he was looking her straight in the face. His pig-like eyes were completely hidden by his unruly eyebrows. 'You ought to be ashamed of yourself,' he declaimed. 'An old woman like you going around showing your thighs like that.'

I can't go on, no matter how much Dolores encourages me. I can't bring myself to tell her he said that, or that that unkind phrase has tormented me for years and made me feel like creeping into a hole in the ground, my face stinging with shame. Especially in front of the boy and girl in jeans. I'd been found guilty of being an impostor and had been exposed in public. All I could manage was to get up from my seat and run out into the street.

'I wanted to get to my brother's, pull on some jeans and a jacket and rush straight out in search of my passport. That and nothing else. Or perhaps I wanted to drop dead on the spot, but that never happens and anyway one doesn't really mean it.'

The girl laughed and poured herself another cup of coffee.

'It's cold. Let me warm it up. I ought to make a fresh lot but I can't be bothered.'

Despite the girl's protestations, the woman pours the coffee back into the pot and goes back into the kitchen. It will give her a chance to get her breath back. Her throat is dry from so much talking. She slowly drains a glass of water. She lifts up the lace curtains in the kitchen window. Her brother's kitchen window had looked out on to an air vent. Facing it, within arm's reach, was a grey wall streaked with long stains left by the rain. She'd opened the window and looked out. At the bottom of the air vent you could see the top of a cage, some bits of junk, a pail and broom with its bristles splayed out in all directions. There was nothing more depressing than an apartment block in Buenos Aires. She'd gone out into the Calle Sarmiento not knowing where to start. The city began to weigh on her and she was beset by forebodings. How had she failed to notice the presence of something lurking beneath the glitter of the cafés, the well-groomed faces of the passersby, the newsstands packed with magazines, that scrubbed odour of elegance and affluence? Supposing she were to buy a paper and find she couldn't understand what it said? Supposing people talked to her in a strange language? It started to rain and she took refuge under an awning in the Calle Lavalle. She felt the warmth seep back into her body; it was the same rain, the same comforting, driving rain she remembered from her childhood, swishing and swirling in the blustery wind. The street turned into a river bobbing with greasy litter from the pizzerias. The smell of open countryside brought by the rain was broken from time to time by an unmistakable whiff of grilled chicken.

She comes back into the room with the hot coffee. The girl is leafing through a book.

You know, Dolores, I'd like to be able to convince you

the world was a fascinating place till a relatively short while ago, when everything became tainted by fear, pain and death. It's hard to imagine now, but such a world did exist. Maybe you never glimpsed it because your resignation was handed down to you by your parents, who from the moment of birth had expected to die and had made ready for the eventuality so it wouldn't catch them unprepared. I've never met your parents, but I can imagine them looking at you. I can see them as if I knew them, their lives taken up with earning a meagre living, queuing to claim their state benefits, making regular visits to the hospital to get their money's worth, even if it meant being operated on for imaginary ills; dressed all year round in sensible colours that wouldn't show the dirt, your father protecting his clothes at work by putting on overalls, your mother by wearing a faded housecoat. I can imagine how they narrowed the horizons you'd have liked to explore. And I feel like giving you a hug when I think that, despite all that, you became a poet, able to invent words and mournful, mysterious landscapes, and to trail them with you untarnished through the desert of everyday existence. I'd like to express such private emotions to you, but the manners acquired over a lifetime have castrated me too; it's not true what people say about my freedom and all that. So I silence my feelings of love and pour out a coffee for you, politely, without spilling a drop, just like they taught me, look, I've even managed to control my shaking hands for the first time since I heard the news from Chile. No one looking at us now would guess that you woke up battered and bruised in a hospital bed, plugged into a tube, because the brutes fancied letting you wake up without the baby and with two or three organs ruptured, rather than let you die and make an end of it; nor that I spend every minute of the day and night imagining variations on the fate of my son and his wife in Santiago: either he's running through the streets dragging her after him, stumbling in her advanced pregnancy, only to run straight into a military patrol; or they're bombing the industrial belts where they've barricaded themselves in and he (or is it she?) is crawling through the rubble, his leg (or arm) gets trapped; or they take them out into the middle of the square and/or force them to dig their own graves; or she's desperately trying (the military close on their heels) to get through a hole he's made in a wire fence; or in the middle of the night they come banging on the door of their hut where... or they simply cart them off to the Stadium, where they say there are hundreds or thousands of people, according to the news; or he gets separated from her in a scuffle and, in the worst option of all, the two of them, on their own, search for each other in vain, weeping and wailing as they trail round the streets, mindless of the curfew; or they're on their way back to the south of the country, when the carriage door bursts open and they point their machine guns at them. Or the two of them with their arms raised, just like when they waved goodbye at the airport, clambering on the wire fence, white-faced, haggard, while she in a gentle voice says 'Don't shoot, comrades' because till her dying breath she'll go on believing everyone is her comrade. And then the world goes up in flames.

'To go back to the subject of Luisa, you know I've never set foot in the Plaza Zabala since, I couldn't bear to. I can't imagine her in Lyons. She's bound to turn up here one of these days. Though something funny happens to those who leave, have you noticed? To start with, they reply to your letters immediately, feeling homesick, and then gradually they start to lose touch. It's only natural, but it's not just that; it's as if they became different people, as if they'd never lived here. I know they've got a right to do what they want with their lives, who'd choose to stay in this dump? But it makes me angry.'

The woman didn't want to pursue that topic. She changed tack by asking after Flaquita and her boyfriend.

'I don't see much of them,' Dolores replied tartly.

'Flaquita only looked about twelve.'

'Heavens! She's only a year younger than me.'

'But she looked like a child. I can see her now turning her head in the Volkswagen to eye me up and down.'

'They're around,' Dolores said after a pause, reluctantly. 'It's just that I can't stomach people like that.'

'Why? What did they do?'

'Nothing. That's the point. Absolutely nothing. When Néstor came out of prison, he and Flaquita took to avoiding us, as if we had the plague. They never spoke to us again, just imagine. And things were going really badly for us at the time. They both got jobs, Flaquita in a bookshop and Néstor as a lawyer's clerk. I've no objection to that, don't get me wrong. What I object to is their disloyalty, not wanting to have anything to do with any of us. Do you think she came to see me when I was in the hospital? Or that they got in touch when it was announced on television that Enrique had been killed?'

'Perhaps they never found out. No one knows what's happened to his next-door neighbour any more.'

'But not when it's broadcast on TV. Besides, we're allowed to talk about the deaths announced on television, unlike the others, because they're officially listed. Even the cat knew when you died on TV, because then you became public domain.'

'Didn't you ever bump into her in the street?'

'Yes, once, she was about twenty yards away from me. She had her little boy with her, clutching her hand, he must be about four by now. And do you know what she did? Drove back past me in the Volkswagen to take a furtive look at me. I call that pretty strange behaviour.'

'Well,' the woman murmured, 'if she's got a child...'

It upset her that Dolores should judge Flaquita so harshly, and it also annoyed her that Flaquita had ignored Dolores. But that was life. One couldn't take sides. The survival instinct always takes over when death is in the offing.

'And besides, what hurt me most was that she should think I wouldn't understand her. When she knew perfectly well

I'd got into this mess because of Enrique and didn't have many ideas of my own to start with. In fact at the beginning they were a bit suspicious of me, because I wanted to write funny, useless things no one understood. Except for Enrique, of course. And I still write the same funny things.'

She smiled.

'Before, I used to write for pleasure, out of vanity, who knows. Now I do it as a defence. It's odd, but poetry is my defence against both life and death. Does that make sense? Because for me the two things are a threat. Writing calms me down, it makes me feel I've left things behind, that I'm on top of them. Don't ask me why I want to feel on top, I've no idea. It's all so complicated. And that's what I think about as I file bits of paper in an office.'

She laughed silently, brushing back a strand of hair that has fallen over her face.

'Where do you work now?'

'It makes no difference. I've worked in lots of offices and they're all the same, full of spiteful idiots. Can you believe that I was already doing office work before I was 15? In the postal service, in a room with rows and rows of desks facing a partitioned office where the boss worked. He spent all his time summoning us, in fact that's all he ever did; and whenever a name was called there'd be the same tense silence. I remember one poor bloke who used to spring to his feet like a jack-in-the-box whenever the boss summoned him, mechanically adjusting the knot of his tie. It's funny to think of men always wearing ties, isn't it? A Frenchman decided to put on a special act the next time the boss called his name, to spoof him. As soon as he heard his name, he stood up, slowly unzipped his fly and zipped it up again. The silly fool thought he was titillating us. There were suppressed giggles all round, and from that day on he took to repeating the exercise, with ever greater success. I used to escape from such crass stupidity by slipping out into the corridors that led to the lavatories. I always used to pray there'd be no one there so I could lean on the windowsill for a bit, but, as usual, no one heard my prayers. The lavatories were always packed with fat dolled-up women, skinny consumptive women, middle-aged women making crochet table mats while they listened to the dirty jokes told by the more brazen amongst them: the female postal workers' zoo. . . ugh! But I managed to get a peep out of the window and glimpse the bare square outside, with its mast sticking up in the middle. One day the boss summoned me, enquired how things were going at school, and then out of the blue asked me if we masturbated in the lavatories. I said yes, of course. I'd no idea what he was talking about but I'd been advised never to disagree with my boss. He looked a little shaken and started to fidget, but as I didn't know what to do next, I asked if that was all and made a quick exit. I forgot about it; some two weeks later something reminded me of the episode and I looked the word up in the dictionary. But I don't know why on earth I'm telling you all this.'

'We were talking about Flaquita and how she's working in an office now.'

'Was that it? No, wait, what I wanted to say was that I've never poked my nose into other people's affairs. I've no objection to them wanting to lead a quiet life with their little boy, dreaming of eating ice cream on Pocitos beach in summer, what's wrong with that? And anyway I'm sure that in the long run things will settle down into a kind of stalemate, which is something Enrique would never have accepted, nor Tomás. Which is why the poor things had their pictures flashed up on TV with numbers hanging round their necks like convicted murderers. That's the reward we got for rejecting their welfare-state paradise. And yet, no matter how irrational it may sound, I'd still reject it if I had to make the choice again. And that's what I can't forgive Flaquita, who was the most dogmatic of us all. Anyway, never mind, I still don't know if they gave you back your wretched passport or not.'

'I went back first thing the following morning. What choice was there? It would have been even worse if I'd got other people involved. The police station didn't open till nine and I spent something like an hour wandering round aimlessly.'

'I love Buenos Aires. There's something special about it for us, you know. For me, anyway.'

'It may be beautiful if you live in a fashionable district like Palermo, but if you live in the south...'

'It's just that you've always hated Buenos Aires.'

'Yes and no. I had my reasons. Growing up as a poor girl in the south of the city is one of the less enviable fates you could wish on anyone. But over the years I've grown reconciled to it. The last few times I was there I quite enjoyed seeing the old haunts again.

'A couple of years or so ago, when I was still making the trip to Buenos Aires, I went to the zoo. It was freezing cold and the poor creatures were huddling in the corners of their cages. Two keepers started to eye me suspiciously because I had my hands in my pockets. I felt like sticking them up, but you can never be sure how a man in a uniform will react nowadays. When I came out into the Plaza Italia, I felt incredibly depressed. But of course by that time we were all feeling the pressure.'

'I can imagine,' the older woman said. 'But five years ago it was still bearable. As I waited for the police headquarters to open, I nosed around the cafés, making silly wagers. If I could count more people dipping their croissants into their coffee than people breaking them with their fingers, they'd give me back my passport. Six people were dipping their croissants, three were breaking them, and four didn't enter into the count, buried in their newspapers. Things looked doubtful. I remembered my grandfather dipping sops into his wine glass at the table and swilling them down with a revolting slurping noise. I found it disgusting and used to make a rude face, not stopping to think that the old man didn't have a single tooth in his mouth. They'd all been pulled out with the first available pair of pliers lying around. The slightest toothache and goodbye tooth.'

'You sound as though you were talking about a medieval

peasant, not your grandfather.'

'What do you expect? We progress quickly in Argentina. One generation standing on the shoulders of the previous one to get a head start. A nation of circus acrobats, that's what we are.'

The nearer it got to nine o'clock, the more nervous she felt. She tried to suppress a tickle in her vagina and an urgent need to pee, because the toilets. . . She always managed to arrange these things badly. Would she have time to get to Lezama Park and back? She calculated it couldn't be more than three blocks away. Her desire to urinate vanished as if by magic. She set off briskly and when, in the distance, she glimpsed a clump of trees belonging to the park, she was overtaken by a savage joy. Once again she would tread those shady paths, she would recognise the line of gravel curving round towards the stone stairway, she would slowly ascend the steps worn away in the middle, testing the dip with her toes. The imposing stairway leading up the hill would present her with its four ritual stopping-off points. First, the bench overgrown by ivy. Second, the half-naked female figure, frozen in a running posture with her marble hair streaming out behind her. Third, the mahogany tree that had been struck by lightning. Through the gap you could see the distant facades of the Calle San Telmo. The little girl would climb the tree and perch on a branch till, ecstatically, she succeeded in making out the distant balcony with its curtains tied back on both sides. She would close her eyes in order to imagine the warmth and comfort that must exist inside, the smell of the carved dressers, the linen tablecloths, the cold touch of the gleaming cutlery. Fourth, the top of the hill, crowned with a thicket of trees. The terrace was lined with intricate wrought-iron benches, with legs ending in lions' paws. The balustrade was so wide she couldn't touch the outer edge. In the distance, the river was the Sargasso Sea, dotted with yellow barges. She stopped short as she turned the corner facing the park. Where was the green dip leading to the steep hill? Why had she ever thought of coming back? She turned on her heels and plunged into the streets as close as winding sheets. Perhaps it was the drizzle, perhaps it was her disturbed state of mind, but she felt there was nowhere in the whole world a grey so dismal as the grey of the south of Buenos Aires.

'I was distraught. Not only did I have to face a third inspector, but a fourth, a fifth, I can't even remember how many! And it's odd because, looking back at it now with hindsight, I think I got off lightly. After all, what was so terrible about having to go from office to office reclaiming a stupid document? Little did I know that a few years later it would be a matter of reclaiming people and not documents, it doesn't bear thinking about; and you wouldn't be able to get near their desks, or even go through the front door of those gloomy buildings, let alone have the privilege of being on the receiving end of their sarcasm and insolence. Little did I know then that the most withering look would be received with boundless gratitude and the most gross insult welcomed as a favour.'

'I've got lost. What are you referring to?'

'I'm talking about the moment they closed their doors and stopped looking at you and answering your questions.'

'Blind, deaf and dumb, what more could you want.'

'But in my case it was a game, of course. They played cat-and-mouse with me for a few days, kept me waiting as long as possible, then tossed me the passport and that was the end of it. But I didn't feel like coming back to Argentina in a hurry again.'

'But you did come back, when things were at their worst. That was a splendid gesture on your part. And just to comfort Elena.'

The woman barely managed to stammer: 'Elena? What Elena?'

'Elena Gordon, Victoria's mother, what's got into you?'

All sorts of things. So Elena Gordon Paz was plain Elena nowadays? She felt irked that her friendship with Elena had been usurped, but the feeling subsided. Just what was the relationship between Dolores, her friend and Victoria?

The girl came to her rescue.

'You probably don't even know I worked with Victoria's group. We'll talk about that later on. But you'd come back for the festival that was banned, isn't that right? I read about it in the papers, despite the fact that with the censorship hardly any news got into print. Of course we heard at the time they'd started to clamp down on people in the theatre; it was a week of threats and expulsions.'

'I left after three days too. Every time the phone rang and I picked it up, it was some attempt at intimidation.'

'Did you go to Lima or Bogotá?'

'To Bogotá, because of Antonio's bank. I'd just married Antonio.'

'What's Antonio like?'

'What's he like? I can't think of what to say. The only thing that comes to mind are the Havana cigars he smokes.'

She laughed openly and the girl couldn't help but laugh with her. Both of them were laughing light-heartedly.

'So why did you do it?' Dolores asked.

'I don't really know the answer to that either. For security. So as not to be alone. Because I'm a coward, who knows. It allowed me to give all my time to the theatre, that matters, doesn't it? He's got two children, the elder of the two is about to have his twenty-fifth birthday, just a year older than my son. We don't see much of them, one is studying in Switzerland, the other in England.'

'Hmm... Just what they wanted for Victoria.'

So we're back to square one. Back to the seventh circle without possibility of escape? Wouldn't it be better if Victoria were in London? And if Enrique and my son...? No, it wouldn't be better. That's one thing I do know for sure, and I know it thanks to my last trip to Buenos Aires. Or perhaps I already knew it on the bus packed with tourists coming back into Argentina after visiting the Iguazú Falls.

You can't imagine what an awful journey it was! With that innocent air and neat, homely look, with their well-cut tailored suits, leather handbags and silk scarves artlessly knotted. Not the slightest hint of sweat, no vulgar boxes of Kleenex, the only people in the world who blow their noses with embroidered hankies, care of Harrods (Buenos Aires). The most unlikely place for me to be attacked by apprehensions and forebodings, that started to mushroom in the most alarming manner. In addition to which I was wrapped up in my own thoughts, lost to the outside world. I was obsessed with the thought of Victoria. Why had all this happened? What was her motive? Why had my friend left her magnificent flat after Victoria's disappearance? It was all a big jumble in my head, and I couldn't help feeling resentfully that it was the fault of those avenging angels that always took it out on you without anyone giving them the go-ahead. Why just now, when the general affluence was there for all to see, with everyone downing kilos of sirloin and mountains of ravioli, overflowing with pride in the national flag, football, the Malvinas, whatever was held up to them as an example? An entire nation cavorting after the carrot dangling in front of their nose, while at the same time people were literally being hacked to pieces, with everyone pretending it had nothing to do with them. That was the overall picture. Some people say Buenos Aires has gone downhill and, what with all those second-generation Galician immigrants and Italians from Abruzzo, it's no longer the slick, brash city it used to be. You wouldn't have thought so on that coach oozing bourgeois smugness. As we drove through the vast, open pampas, its passengers swapped postcards and promised to send each other the obligatory snaps they'd taken amid the foaming waters of the falls.

There was nothing to look at on either side of the road. Absolutely nothing for miles and miles on end. It's hard to believe such an empty country can exist. From time to time, as the coach rolled on and on, I would feel old hatreds stirring inside me; against my teachers at school, against the cattle, against my immigrant grandparents, against the aunts in the photograph, against myself. Against myself because, in this perfect jigsaw, some pieces did not belong: where did the torturers, the informers, the murderers fit in?

We got out at a wayside café to stretch our legs and have a coffee and croissant. The women made for the toilets, discreetly, for in spite of that veneer of elegance, English schooling and winning the World Cup, everyone knows they're filthy and there's not an inch of clean floor you can put your foot on. Let alone your arse. Ladies and little girls roll up their trouser legs and come out with an unmistakable look of distaste on their faces; but no sooner are they seated round the table, giving orders to the balding, flat-footed waiter, than at the drop of a hat they recover their self-assurance. And I take part in the conversation and smiles, polite to the last, I compare postcards, plunge into the collective cup of coffee that makes the world a more pleasant place to live in. All of a sudden a girl comes up to me with a peaked cap on saying ARGENTINA THE GREATEST. And isn't the girl with her holding a can with the national flag on it? I start to look at the kids around me; they've all got little flags, badges, T-shirts, caps saying I LOVE ARGENTINA, WE ARE THE CHAMPIONS. They're all champions, each and every one of them. 'Do you like football?' I ask a little girl who can't be more than eight. 'Hate it,' she says screwing her face up rudely, 'but we're the champions.' 'Champions at what?' I ask, to stir things up a bit. But I can feel everyone fall silent around me. 'Champions at everything,' one of the mothers replies, with a taut smile. The best football, the best meat, the best education system. I think to myself, 'She's going to say the best government,' but she ends the list there. Still, I bet she thought it. We drive off into the fog bound for Rosario, but I can't stop looking around me at my travelling companions. How had I managed not to notice they were the champions? How had I managed not to hear the songs they've been singing all the way? How had I failed to register their triumphal tone, their aggressive manner, the knowing looks, the Olympic coaching they've all received, men, women and children? Argentina *über alles*; a shiver runs down my spine. At that point the coach slowed down and the road ahead took on a menacing look. The merrymaking died down. The coach slowly pulled in to a police checkpoint. Through the glass you could see the driver and his assistant talking to several people in uniform. I felt envious of the woman to my right who went on blithely playing cards, while my heart pounded wildly. Outside, the driver's mate was jumping up and down to keep warm, but a rap on the shoulder from the driver brought him to a hasty standstill. When they climbed back into the coach the driver turned to face the passengers, raised his voice and announced that we had to take a detour to avoid going through Rosario. It was obvious there was trouble in Rosario, but no one asked what was going on. 'It must be a fire,' one of the card players declared in a loud voice. A feigned sense of relief ran round the coach. 'That'll give us more time to learn the songs by heart,' another voice said. The words ARGENTINA THE BRAVE blasted out agressively; but the voices failed to cohere. I thought that if I hadn't been there, they'd all have been talking about the enemies of the people. I was the Jew on the coach, I'd sown discord and unrest amongst them. The little girl with the cap was looking at me out of the corner of her eye. She stood in the aisle next to me and started to bawl: 'As Apollo's rays on high appear,' eyeing me as she sang the patriotic song. She stopped and asked me crossly: 'Don't you know the words?' I said I did but didn't feel like singing. 'Why not?' she snapped back. The people around me were starting to prick up their ears. I was appalled that a snotty little brat should be interrogating me like this; without more ado I ought to tell her I'd have thought her mother would have taught her better manners, but her mother was probably waiting to prove me wrong.

'I bet you said nothing of the sort.'

'Quite right. Not only did I hold my tongue but I said I had a sore throat and even patted her silly little World Cup hat.'

' "The sound of clashing steel draws near",' Dolores hummed. 'And can you tell me what made you go back to Buenos Aires, when things were at their worst?'

'I'd got it into my head that I had to see Elena. How could I have said what I felt about something like that in a letter?'

'Did she ask you to come?'

'She'd never have done that, she never said a word about it. I only found out through other people. But from the moment they told me she went to the Plaza de Mayo every Thursday, I knew I just had to be with her, even if it was only once.'

'It's curious. Though it's typical of you too; I'd expect that kind of gesture from you. And then you'd been very close when you were young, hadn't you?'

'Best friends, sisters even. The kind of intimacy you know only once in a lifetime. We did everything together, we collected and hoarded memories.'

'What?' the girl asked.

She looked through her rather than at her. She couldn't possibly understand. How could she explain that you could collect things like walking round a river bend, a tree top seen from below one summer's day, the gleam of something tinny in the dark; a certain one-and-only look, the touch of a hand, both of you starting to laugh at the same time, going into the classroom one particular day, water splashing against the side of the boat, someone sobbing uncontrollably, Scarlet O'Hara falling down the stairs, silly details fixed forever because both girls looked at them from the same point of view, birds being shot down and plummeting on to the tree tops in the early evening, fear of the dark, footsteps, threatening hisses . . . Maybe it was because of all those things that she was on this crowded coach; because of them and not because of anyone's struggle against anyone else, who knows.

With any luck we'd arrive in the early hours of the morning. If they didn't mow us down with their machine guns on the way, in which case we'd never know who'd killed us or why, as happens so often nowadays. But there was no point being melodramatic. The driver picked up his microphone and suggested that the ladies and gentlemen might like to sleep for a while instead of shouting and screaming. He didn't put it quite like that but that was what he meant. Clearly put out, the daytrippers from Igauzú took a break and switched to whispering with their heads leaning against the back of their seats. They'd missed seeing a town on the way and now they couldn't even sing; all because of those delinquents, as usual, the enemies of the fatherland who insisted on continuing the dirty war. As if reading their minds, the driver turned the lights off, but the impression of tranquility was purely superficial for you could sense the pent-up hatred. The girl with the little peaked cap squatted in the aisle beside me, muttering: 'It's all because of those troublemakers that we've missed seeing Rosario.' I pretended to be asleep, but I was suddenly made aware that this coach trip was forcing me to take sides and had placed me in a definite position. I was on a different side from the other passengers. I had nothing to do with them, I hadn't even set out with the idea in mind; but it was clear that they were my enemies. The uncertainty of not being sure what life was like on this new side of the fence unnerved me totally. All of a sudden, I felt hatred and was the object of the hatred of others. Boring people who before I'd dismissed as inoffensive now turned out to have a hidden, dangerous side; beneath the painted hearts, the flags of victory, the innocent T-shirts, a sinister symbolism was at work. Not feeling enthusiastic about football could, it seemed, be construed a crime punishable by death. The little girl with the peaked cap would whisper in the ear of the driver, who would whisper in the ear of the policeman at the checkpoint, who would whisper in the ear of the inspector on duty, who would whisper in the ear of the torturers.

Drained by terror I fell asleep, till the coach braked sharply and the driver announced that we were entering the outskirts of Buenos Aires. It was getting light; I sat up in my seat and looked at the people around me. They were sleeping in the most extraordinarily composed positions. Nothing could unsettle them. In the next seat, a young lady primly took out a thermos and poured a cup of coffee, which she proceeded to sip with evident relish. I felt like asking her what she thought about the Thursday demonstrations in the Plaza de Mayo, but I recalled all the things my friends, worried by my clandestine entry into the country, had said about the need to be prudent. We drove through interminable industrial suburbs, after leaving behind the bungalows with their gardens and fences. Every now and then a purple neon sign would shimmer, and a haggard face would look out of an undertaker's window. No city in the world managed to be so utterly depressing. Despite all my years of familiarity with the systematic greyness of life in Buenos Aires, I felt incredibly saddened. At the same time, I was disarmed by this vast, sprawling, provincial city. For some reason, what most disarmed me were the bakeries where they must be taking trays of fresh bread and buns out of the oven. The coach plunged into a virtual tunnel of mahogany trees; women were already coming out to scrub the marble front doorsteps.

'Well, well,' said Dolores laughing. 'And you have the nerve to say you hate Buenos Aires!'

She tossed her hair back and pushed it behind her ears. I was staggered by the superb bone-structure of her face. How had I managed not to notice she could be beautiful? She went on laughing for she knew that, whatever I might say, I could never get away from Buenos Aires.

'But I do hate it, really. Everything about the place drives me up the wall. Immediately on arrival at the Plaza Once, I was confronted by a perfect example of Argentine manhood when some brute ran out and kicked my bag. You can't imagine how dreadful the station was, a real dump.'

'Like any bus station anywhere in the world, what do you expect?'

'No, it was worse. I had to walk through a carpet of greasy litter from the nearby take-away foodstands. The smell of which attracted hordes of dogs roaming among the suitcases and porters. Such details are unimportant, I know, but things like that get me down because they make me start to question my stupid behaviour. It was idiotic to have come back; a crazy idea, doomed from the outset.'

They fell silent.

'Do you often have that feeling? That you've got things completely wrong?'

'I'm not quite sure what you mean by "got things wrong". Not with trivial things like that. For us there was only one possible thing you could get wrong, and that was not getting involved in what was going on. The truth is we didn't stop to think about other possible mistakes. I mean, things like whether it had been a mistake to marry this person instead of that, to have children or not, to live here rather than there, none of that seemed particularly important. What I mean is that our lives, as such, are not particularly important. I'll go even further: Enrique and I were together, but I could probably just as well have lived with Juan; and Enrique with Flaquita, for example.'

She was taken aback by her tone of voice and felt obliged to take a defensive stand, because that wasn't where she'd been leading at all. 'She'll come straight out with it any minute now,' she thought. And all she'd wanted was to confess her constant changes of mind and the self-doubts that continually plagued her, thinking her instability was an adolescent feature that brought her close to young people. If it was true that being mature meant always knowing what you were doing, then no one was less mature than herself.

She felt hurt by the girl's aggressive manner. She saw that she'd picked up St. Barbara again and had gone back to playing with the statue's wooden arm. What kind of relationship had she had with Elena? With Victoria it was understandable; but with Elena? It was impossible to imagine two people more different from each other. Even she, despite their closeness, had often been unable to repress a feeling of irritation and even envy at Elena's starched school uniform, her chauffeur-driven car, her mother absent-mindedly toying with her pearl necklace, Elena's application in class, her fur-lined winter boots, her way of dancing while holding her partner at arm's length, the gleam of her hair, the photos of Elena in society magazines, Elena's riding outfit; how could a girl like Dolores relate to such out-and-out, all-round sophistication?

She imagined she must have been rather like Dolores, as far as her gaucheness and shabby clothes were concerned, when she met up with Elena again in Paris. And although Elena, with her usual discreet elegance, had played the role of the student waiting for the next check to arrive, she was still superlative in every respect; in the street, at university, in the cafés, in the small circle of euphoric, happy-go-lucky, starving Latins in what was one of the worst European winters on record. And then all of a sudden, to complete the picture, love at first sight, all-engrossing and ecstatic, with the perfect match; the most promising young student of all, from a good family, who was expected to graduate with honours from the venerable medical school at the end of the year. Abel was notorious, among other things, for the little black notebook he carried around with him wherever he went. He would meticulously jot down every outgoing, no matter how small. He stoically put up with the teasing to which he was subjected by all and sundry, particularly during the first half of the month. From that point on, when the meals became more scarce and people started scrounging off one another, it was he who did the teasing, playfully getting his own back. In the beginning he treated her with a special deference on account of her close friendship with Elena, but things started to deteriorate when she set up with the painter who would later become her husband and, at the same time, decided she wanted to go in for the theatre. Elena also became more distant, as though both decisions were a kind of betrayal. They rapidly grew apart. She went on trying to salvage their friendship, but her visits to the tiny apartment where Elena and Abel set up home were not a success. Even the birth of Victoria did little to improve things; she went to see her a month afterwards; Elena was tiptoing round the apartment because at the time Abel was preparing for his final examinations. Victoria was asleep in a tiny cot next to the round table where they ate, so as not to disturb Abel. It was unbelievable how Elena could wind her way in and out of the furniture without upsetting anything.

'I decided to stop seeing the two of them, they'd shown their true Argentinian colours. But as I wandered round the streets of Paris, I realised tears were running down my cheeks. It wasn't the cold. It was a deep-rooted yet quite irrational anger, didn't they have the right to choose their way of life as I'd chosen mine? But no matter how much I tried to be rational, I couldn't come to terms with it. And I was even more upset when I learnt they'd left Paris while I was away in London with the painter. They left a laconic note for me with friends; Abel had qualified as a doctor, the time had come to go back to Buenos Aires. They were sorry to leave Europe, but thought it was for the best. They hoped to see me sometime in Buenos Aires. The note was signed by both of them, but Elena had added a postscript. ''I'll always want to hear from you. Don't lose touch.'' So. The image came back to me of how she'd run across the Place Saint-Sulpice in the freezing, pouring rain to fling her arms around me, after getting married in the sacristy. We were waiting outside, jumping up and down, because we didn't believe in marriage or the Church and perhaps also because, deep down, I was jealous and resentful of Abel. That's the story of our friendship, which was followed by a gap of twenty years, or nearly. Just imagine.'

'But you said you kept in touch by letter, at least.'

'Yes, we wrote to each other, not all that often but fairly regularly. On the birth of her second child and my first one, whenever we moved to another city; I mean whenever my husband and I moved, because they settled in Buenos Aires. But when I got divorced, her letters became more frequent and also more intimate. It was a bad patch in my life, when I was going through a series of depressions and upheavals. I was having rows all the time with my son.'

'Were you in Lima?'

'No, in Bogotá.'

The girl got up and leant on the mantelpiece. She ought to give her the chance to tell her how she'd got to know Elena, but what could she do if she stayed silent and it was so hard to get a word out of her. To be honest, she was less interested in listening to Dolores than in listening to herself; she'd opened the floodgates and there was no way of shutting them. She had a vague feeling that going over things, going back in time would throw some light on her present situation. What she did know for certain was that talking about things was not an escape from the present. On the contrary, it was a kind of peg on which the present hung and which somehow made it possible to cope. The fact that others had been through the same hell gave her the strength to endure it. Maybe hell was not a temporary state but a new way of life. Stop it, what was she saying . . . She mustn't jump to unwarranted conclusions; the best thing was to keep going over things in her head. She'd take advantage of Dolores' silence to try to put events in some kind of order.

The servants came to the door of the penthouse in the Avenida Alvear. As soon as she set foot inside the hall, she was beset by the feeling that everything was perfect and in some curious way definitive. She would have liked to look round her at the vast drawing room divided into different living areas, each arranged round a particular object and item of furniture, but Elena came in straightaway. She hadn't changed at all, she advanced across the room as though the objects around her didn't exist, she spoke with the same fresh, deliberate voice, she had the same half-bemused, half-condescending smile. The same person, as she ushered me to the appropriate seat, telling me how her son was studying medicine and how Victoria was about to graduate in biology. The same person, as she eagerly asked about my son and how was he getting on in Chile? He must meet Victoria some day, they'd have to get to know each other. I couldn't quite see why it was so important that they should meet. I told her he liked being in Chile, and yes, we got on a lot better now; he was living with a Bolivian girl and had no plans to return to Bogotá. She began to pour out the tea, deftly handling the bone-china teacups as if they were surgical instruments. Had the famous medical specialist trained her? Or was it she who'd trained Abel? She drew me out of my self-absorption by persisting with her questions about my son. Why had he left a country where things were nice and quiet for one where, right now at least, everything seemed to be in chaos? Did he belong to a political party? I was surprised by the slight note of anxiety in her voice as she questioned me about a boy she'd never met. It was at that point that Victoria came into the room. I was dazzled by her breathtaking good looks, but I noticed straightaway that she carried them in much the same way as her mother handled the teacups; slightly embarrassed about them and as if trying to play them down. After the usual exchange of pleasantries, she also showed great interest in hearing what my son was doing in Chile. We went back to discussing careers and the relative merits of this and that, and she fell silent as her mother and I discussed whether architecture was better than anthropology. She suddenly excused herself and left the room. I couldn't help commenting on how beautiful she was. Elena smiled and had to admit that she left a trail of admiration behind her wherever she went despite the fact that she was dressed so scruffily, girls

nowadays, you know. 'But don't think I mind,' she blurted
out. 'That sort of comment doesn't do her justice.' She looked
thoughtful. I asked after Abel and her son. Oh, she hardly
ever saw them, they were so busy with their work that they
hardly had time for anything: she couldn't understand why
Abel kept accepting the presidency of so many institutions.
And her son was following in his father's footsteps. 'They
think no one can manage without them,' she smiled teasingly.
At least they'd so far always managed to spend Christmas
together in New York or London. They had a modest apartment in each city and hoped their offspring would take
advantage of this fact to do their doctorates abroad. When
it was time for me to go, I felt like backing out of the door,
so as not to lose one minute of that vision of perfect bliss.
But I restrained myself and merely gave her a warm hug.
Both of us were feeling somewhat emotional, it was silly
really. I went down in the lift thinking how incredible, no
one had been able to take away from us the experiences we'd
shared.

Dolores edged away from the mantelpiece and, lowering her
voice, asked if she was expecting someone. No, nobody. The
doorbell rang again, piercingly. She really must get round
to changing it for one that was less shrill. She got up to go
to the door but the girl grabbed her by the arm; she looked
at her and was taken aback. The colour had drained from
her face and the two purple rings under her eyes made her
look like a corpse. The two of them stood rooted to the
ground.
    'Who are you expecting?' Dolores asked again in a
whisper.
    'No one, I swear.'
    She thought her hushed tone sounded ridiculous. Neither
of them moved or spoke. But when it rang again, the girl
did something that startled her; she fell to her knees and buried
her head in the folds of the older woman's skirt.

'Don't go to the door,' she whispered. 'If you're not expecting anyone, please don't go to the door, I beg you.'

She tilted the girl's head upwards to reason with her and saw something she'd never seen before. Fear disfiguring a face. When the bell rang for the third time, she realised she too was in danger of succumbing. She made an effort to pull herself together and managed gently to extricate herself from the girl, slip off her shoes and tiptoe noiselessly to the door so she could peer through the peephole. She couldn't see anyone. The person ringing the bell must be standing to one side. Deliberately? A shiver ran down her spine. She went back to the sitting room and rested the girl's head between her legs again. She was as limp as a rag doll. The fourth ring of the bell jerked the woman back to her senses and she started to analyse the situation. Hardly anyone knew she was in Montevideo, but if Dolores had found out... And how had she found out? Perhaps she was still involved in something and they'd followed her... This time there was a longer pause, but there was no sound of anyone going down the steps, which meant that the man, or whoever it was, must still be standing beside the door. With his ear to it, listening? At that moment she heard a few hurried footsteps. She let go of the girl again and ran over to the side of the window. A stranger was standing on the pavement, looking in the direction of the house. She beckoned to the girl to come close so she could point him out. She got up awkwardly and stood behind her. No, she'd never seen him. The man crossed the road and got into a car parked a short distance away. Someone at the wheel drove off at top speed.

'Now we'll never know who it was,' the woman said almost reproachfully.

'I know it might have been something quite harmless. But I can't help it, the fear overwhelms me. I can't break the habit. For years we wouldn't open the door to strangers or to anyone who didn't ring with a special code. Do you know what it means to let those bastards in and have them smash everything up, or rush in and hustle you out of the door, or riddle you with bullets before you know what's going on?'

'What's got into you?' she exclaimed, trying to make light of the matter. 'Supposing it was some poor fellow selling bits of whalebone to put in shirt collars?'

'Cut the bad jokes. When did you last see a door-to-door salesman? They've disappeared off the face of the earth. And you can't expect me to believe that a man who comes in a car is selling haircombs. And anyway, why didn't he park outside the house?'

'Stop getting paranoid. You know as well as I do that things have been quiet for some time now.'

'Sure things are quiet now; what with one thing and another they've eliminated everyone there was to eliminate. But what about the people they trained to loot and kill, have you thought about that? What happens to the torturers once they've done themselves out of a job?'

'That's something I've wondered about many a time, believe you me. What do you do with the death squads when you've run out of victims?'

They looked at each other unable to speak. Life becomes unbearable when you can't think of an answer.

'They don't go away,' Dolores finally replied. 'Nor does fear; there's no way of getting rid of it.'

'It sounds an embarrassingly arrogant thing to say; but I've never felt fear. I don't know what the word means. Even these last few days I couldn't put a name to what I've felt. It's as though the anguish of having no news about my son were all around me, seeping into me. Is that what fear is? I knew I was *persona non grata* in Buenos Aires, but I wasn't afraid to return. I wasn't afraid to go to the Plaza de Mayo with her either. Maybe I just don't stop to think.'

'I don't know. What I do know is that you don't feel afraid as long as you go on believing there are certain things that can't happen to you. You hear about them killing other people, torturing them, maiming them; but you think it's got nothing to do with you. Fear starts when it touches you personally and you realise you were wrong, that you're not immune.'

Now they were pacing up and down the sitting room, leaning on the backs of the armchairs, absent-mindedly deciphering the titles of the books on the shelves, peering out of the windows or the doors leading on to the patio. With a jolt the thought struck her that the girl had had enough and wanted to leave.

No, you can't go yet, not till I've seen Elena again. I had the address jotted on a scrap of paper which I had to keep consulting to check I'd got it right. At that point the Calle San Martín started to slope down towards the port and it had a somewhat insalubrious look about it. Had I made a mistake? There was nothing specifically sordid you could pinpoint, just that feeling of irremediable, creeping dilapidation. I saw several shops selling leather goods, their windows covered with grime. So much for Argentina's famous cattle . . . Over the door of a seedy bar, next to a tattered awning, were the letters PUB cut out of tinfoil. I went inside and examined the various notices pinned on the wall by the doorway. Straightaway a huge poster caught my eye with the name FOTO-RAP, and next to it a red zigzag arrow pointing towards the stairs. I recalled that in a letter Elena had described the apartment to me and had mentioned some dreadful photographer's studio. So that was it and that was where she was. As I was going up the stairs I suddenly had the sensation of being back in Paris with her; I felt a rush of happiness that made me forget the tragic reason for my visit.

We embraced without making any attempt to conceal our emotion. Then I gave a furtive glance around me at the apartment whose bleakness made it feel much like a Paris studio, though I instantly spotted the orderly touches she always gave to the world around her. I saw the tears well up suddenly in her eyes and I too was unable to hold them back. Wasn't it better to cry now, pointlessly, while we still had some hope of finding her? But we soon calmed down, possibly for that very reason, because we felt ashamed of crying as if we'd

73

given her up for dead. Or perhaps we should? With so many terrible stories going round, there seemed little room for hope. I began to appreciate that the worst torment devised in this new country that had sprung itself on us was the impossibility of finding out what had happened to people. I felt so overwhelmed by the realisation that the sight of Elena standing there, as discreetly elegant as ever, seemed almost unbearable. But then, when I looked at her more closely, I noticed she was emaciated, gaunt, and I could see the toll taken by the sleepless nights and the unbroken anguish since the moment they'd rapped on the door (with the butts of the revolvers as was their custom), and had dragged her off after the violent scene she must have relived a thousand times. Hadn't she tried to tell me over the phone, when I'd rung from abroad to say I was coming to see her? How many times had she re-enacted the story engraved in her memory, perfecting the details? And now she was telling it to me all over again, accosting me as soon as I came in the door, forgetting I'd already heard it from beginning to end. It dawned on me that they'd dealt her the killing blow, as they stun a cow on entering the slaughterhouse, not when they took her away but later on, when no one, anywhere she went, in any office, would admit to having seen her or known her or filed her name or imprisoned her or interrogated her; no one had ever set eyes on her, she never went through the door of any police station, she never went down any corridor, they never kept her standing for hours on end in front of anyone, they never moved her from place to place, they never bundled her into any car without a number plate, they never threw her into any cell, they never entered her name on any list. Never heard of the girl. Some of them, Elena said, flatly refused to look at the photograph. Sinister figures would shake their heads, scratch them, make clucking noises or, worst of all, smile blankly. She probably never existed. But what about her identity card, her passport, the marriage certificate of such eminent parents, the photographs? None of that means a thing, especially nowadays. The enemies of the fatherland are capable of falsifying anything, didn't you know?

And if it was true that she was her mother, then it was up to her to find out where she was. God knows what she might have got up to, knowing the way children were brought up in this day and age; the replies would oscillate between gross insults and paternal advice. And what about Abel's top-level friends? She shuddered. So much for friendship. Their first reaction had been to refuse to see her. At best, she would be admitted to a desk piled high with papers which some official would keep shuffling uneasily, without inviting her to sit down. No, her name was not on any list of detainees in his possession. Perhaps it was on some other list, he'd no way of knowing; how can you find a needle in a haystack? She tells me that phrase was said to her more than once, which shows that those in authority have no imagination. And each time she insisted that a twenty-year-old girl is not a needle nor Buenos Aires a haystack. Whereupon they would look at her wide-eyed; did she mean to say she hadn't noticed that Buenos Aires was not what it used to be? The occasional bureaucrat, full of his own importance, would laugh out loud at his little wisecrack.

As she goes over to the Primus stove to make some coffee, I become aware of an absence I daren't ask her about. Why is she living alone? What about Abel?

I know she'll tell me about it in due course. With her back to me, she waits patiently and silently for the coffee to percolate.

The image of Victoria's luxuriant golden hair flashes into my mind. She'd written to me some time before saying how worried she was about Victoria, without any prior warning, she'd dropped out of university and was moving in undesirable circles. She'd mentioned it in a guarded, almost offhand manner; she must have been seriously alarmed to let the words slip out at all. I had no idea what Victoria was mixed up in till, quite out of the blue, I received a letter from her. We'd only ever met for ten to fifteen minutes over the silver tea service and steaming scones, so it took me completely by surprise. Even more so when I read it. It was a magnificent letter. It started by asking politely if I could possibly do her an enormous favour, since I was the only person she knew in Bogotá. It was a complicated matter, only half explained. I was to receive a visit from someone who, with new documents which I was to procure, was to go on to Central America. The letter was delivered by hand, I never discovered by whom. But after this tactful, formally worded request, the letter launched into a passionate outpouring wanting me to share in the happiness she'd discovered in her new way of life. I looked for clues that might point to a boyfriend, but the happiness she was referring to was of an abstract nature, something akin to the discovery of what this earthly life is all about. Now she knew and her conviction sounded genuine. My immediate reaction was to try to visualise the scenes that must have taken place in the Buenos Aires penthouse if, as seemed to be the case, Victoria had been quite open about her new existence. My friend might be a genius at the art of self-composure, but something like this could not possibly have entered into her calculations. I realised it was Elena, and not Victoria, that mattered to me. And the trouble is that Elena mattered to me because, in a sense, her situation mirrored my own, with a son of roughly the same age about to leave home for Chile, notwithstanding my worries and misgivings. My supposition that a major family rift had occurred was confirmed shortly afterwards by a letter from Elena saying her daughter had moved out to an apartment in the Calle San Martín. I felt a sense of relief, thinking that peace had descended once more on the cut glass in the penthouse. It would all blow over; it wasn't the first or last time a girl had wanted to establish her independence from her parents.

While her friend poured the coffee into two chipped cups, she surveyed the apartment around her. The whole situation was hard to believe. The tenants of the apartment were in Paris; Victoria had disappeared; and Elena, of all people, had taken over this cold, dingy attic. At what point had she decided to move here? Was she taking her daughter's place in order to keep her alive? A platform had been built halfway across the high ceiling, forming a kind of mezzanine with a wooden ladder leading up to it. Looking at it from below, the platform seemed wide enough for little more than a bed. It was a silly thought, but where did she hang her clothes? There was no wardrobe in evidence. Next to us was a coffee table with two chairs, and at the other end of the room the dining table with the Primus stove and a few plates, cups and glasses. The far wall was at an angle and had been partitioned off with a flowery curtain, hiding a door which presumably led to the bathroom. If there was a bathroom. The walls were literally papered with political posters. Had she kept them up as a gesture of defiance? She probably no longer even cared. Maybe she'd been driven to take Victoria's place by some obscure kind of death-wish. Sooner or later the butts of their revolvers would break down that flimsy door. The people in the photographer's studio could easily be informers. The apartment had already been searched once a few months before, fortunately when Victoria was out.

'That was why she suddenly turned up at home, you see. They took away all the books and smashed up everything in sight. One of those death squads.'

'So Victoria moved back in with you?'

'Good heavens, no, she'd never have done that. She came back to give me a parcel that was very important and mustn't be allowed to fall into their hands at any price.'

'Let me get things straight. Do you mean to say it happened the same day she came back?'

'The very same day, precisely; they were obviously watching for her outside the house.'

'She must have trusted you to ask you a favour like that.'

'Yes, she did and rightly so, though she never explained to me what it was she was involved in. Perhaps she realised I'd given her my blessing or rather that I hadn't even stopped to think I might not give my blessing to whatever she chose to do with her life. I know what you're thinking; but you're wrong. It wasn't just to smooth things over. It was because I suddenly realised . . . I don't know what I suddenly realised.'

She went quiet for a moment, as if she still didn't know and it depressed her terribly.

'If only Abel hadn't happened to choose that precise moment to come in through the other door! The three of us froze. Victoria went red, I clasped the parcel she'd given me, and he started to look us up and down, taking his time, trying to figure out what was going on. But he couldn't stop himself, the words came flooding out despite his efforts at self-control. He clearly couldn't take any more. He'd been a changed man ever since Victoria left home.'

She spoke the words sadly, without resentment. I tried to find a soothing phrase; she knew him all too well. If the slightest disruption was enough to upset him, it was hardly surprising he'd found it difficult to come to terms with Victoria's leaving.

She stared at me for a second, but her mind had already gone on to something else.

'Of course. But the scene was awful, you can't imagine. I can't find the words to describe it to you. Abel talked as if he were reciting a speech from memory; he accused Victoria of being irresponsible, or didn't she appreciate the difficult situation she was putting him in? Didn't she understand that his reputation and career were in jeopardy all because of the way she was behaving? Or did she think people were stupid and didn't know what was going on? And while she was playing at revolution — and revolution in the name of what, for God's sake? — he was the one who was having to pay. And there she was without a care in the world or any thought for him. Victoria just stood there staring at him, speechless, blinking back the tears. I think she understood him and felt sorry for him, though she couldn't agree with his way of seeing things. Because Victoria's way of seeing things was no longer ours. And to think that if he hadn't gone on with that interminable string of accusations, none of this would have happened.'

She brushed her forehead as if sweeping back a loose hair, but there was no loose hair to sweep back. A long, lean, transparent hand, with no rings on it.

'Do you realise what I'm saying? If Abel hadn't come in, I'd have had time to take the parcel into another room and hide it.'

So the moment had come for me to hear it all over again.

'Because it was then that they arrived. It was dreadful. When they banged on the door like that, I was paralysed. I don't know what it was that nailed me to the floor. I think I imagined that if I went out of the room I wouldn't be able to defend Victoria. How could I have been so naive? Victoria made no attempt to move either. She'd turned as white as a sheet and her eyes were glued to the door. Abel went to the door and opened it. He acted quite calmly, but the men burst in without any respect. They were looking for this girl, they didn't care a damn if the owner of the house had friends in high places. Victoria made a slight move and they grabbed her by the arms. Abel asked the name of the officer in charge and demanded to see the search warrant. One of them came out with an obscenity by way of reply. He looked at me and said, ''That parcel, let me see it.'' But I clutched it as tightly as I could and we wrestled for a second. ''If you please,'' Abel said, ''this matter will be cleared up without any fuss. My wife will give you the parcel which belongs to my daughter.'' That was when Victoria broke free yelling no, don't give it to him, but she didn't get to me because they already had her pinned on the floor and were punching her and kicking her, and at that point I hurled the parcel to the ground and flew at the men who were hitting her, pummelling them with my fists, completely beside myself. I don't know how long for. One minute, five minutes? They dragged Victoria off struggling and screaming. The officer had the parcel under his arm as he went out of the door. I caught a glimpse of Abel standing ashen-faced in the middle of the room, with his hand outstretched, saying, ''Please, gentlemen, please,'' not making any move to intervene. And behind him, in the corridor that led to the bedrooms, stood her brother, looking on without a word, can you imagine? Keeping at a safe distance, without so much as a single word.'

She started to shake so violently she had to rest the coffee cup on the table. She clutched her head with both hands.

'Victoria was shouting something, but I couldn't hear what. They were the last words she said to me and I couldn't hear them, can you imagine that?'

Yes, I could imagine it. But why had she said last words? One day she and Victoria would recall the whole episode together; and Victoria would probably remember what she'd shouted. And they'd have a good laugh over it. She'd see how they'd have a good laugh over it.

At that point she raised her head and stared at me. The tears were trickling over her lips. It was the face of someone who has given up, of someone who has no more hope or reason for living.

'Ah,' the sound came from her mouth. And again, 'Ah, ah,' like a protracted moan.

'Poor Elena', said Dolores. 'She must have found it a relief to keep going over the scene again and again. You know, I find it hard to understand. I don't want to remember anything. The past is behind me. It's dead and buried. I hate to think what it would be like if I kept replaying it in my mind every day.'

'It's different, you're still a girl.'

'A girl with a great future. To save you the trouble of saying it. No, seriously. I've already said I don't have a future, but I don't want a past either. I couldn't cope with it, it's as simple as that.'

'Don't be silly. No one can float in a vacuum.'

'We are floating in a vacuum,' she exclaimed with a cynical laugh. The phrase appealed to her. 'That's exactly it, floating in a vacuum. But we've had it, who cares anyway. I'd rather you told me what the devil you got up to in the Plaza de Mayo. I've never been, wild horses wouldn't drag me back to Buenos Aires; but some people from our group went and were really upset by it.'

Four o'clock. Half an hour to go before the demonstration started. She briefly explained to me how she'd first met the 'Madwomen of the Plaza de Mayo'. On her interminable, harrowing visits to law courts, police stations, prison waiting rooms, she began to notice she was always coming across the same people. To start with she thought they were following her, but after a while, when she looked more carefully at various women she kept encountering again and again, she realised her suspicions were unfounded. Haggard, wan, those faces reflected her own despair. How could she fail to recognise the signs of that night-long pacing round and round a room on the verge of breakdown? On one occasion, a woman she'd bumped into three times that same day invited her to go for a coffee, and they got talking; when Elena learnt that for some women the search had gone on for years, and that in the case of the woman she was talking to it had been nearly a year and a half, she thought she was going out of her mind. She was feeling very weak; her head began to spin and she had to clutch at the edge of the table to stop herself fainting. The other woman felt sorry for her and gave her her phone number, in case she wanted to join the protest. She heard, dimly, that they met every Thursday in the Plaza de Mayo carrying photographs and lists of names of those who had disappeared. That evening, she staggered back to the empty apartment in the Calle San Martín. She spent several days in bed, barely stirring; every now and then she would climb down to make some coffee and nibble a biscuit. Everything she ate, she vomited. But one morning she woke up to the realisation that, if she went on like that, she was never going to find Victoria, and to give up the search was tantamount to signing her death warrant. She got out the woman's phone number and dialled. The woman's voice sounded flat. No, she hadn't made any progress. She'd had a good-quality enlargement made of her son and took it with her every Thursday. He looked really smart in his school uniform; it had been taken the day he left school, just two weeks before.

Suddenly the voice at the end of the phone perked up; she was really pleased she'd decided to join them, she must let her have her daughter's name so she could add it to the stencilled lists, and her photo too for their records. Did she know how to knit?

'No,' Elena gulped. What a pity, because there was a big group of them that knitted all sorts of things; then they raffled them to raise money for those women whose husbands had disappeared, or for the grandparents who'd been left looking after the babies. Elena wanted to ask 'What babies?' but kept quiet. 'It's better to be on a list than to be nowhere,' the voice concluded. It was a Wednesday. The following day she went to the Plaza de Mayo for the first time, and since then had not missed a week.

'We've got time for one last cup of coffee. It's only a few blocks away.' She got up gracefully and went to light the stove again.

For some time she'd been waiting to ask her something but couldn't pluck up the courage. She didn't quite know how to put it either. She would have liked her to provide an explanation — any explanation — that made sense of Victoria's behaviour. But who was she thinking of: Victoria? Or her son whose letters from Chile were increasingly enthusiastic but increasingly vague about the one thing that mattered to her, that is, how he was getting on at university? She couldn't bring herself to accept that he might lose interest in his research and devote all his energies to politics. It wasn't that she objected to what he was doing, any more than she'd objected to what Victoria had done. It was just that she didn't understand them. She couldn't see the point of their relinquishing their hard-won positions in a society that had time only for winners. In Victoria's case, she was clearly going all-out to lose. And how could a loser win the revolution? She was completely stuck for an answer, she always had been. A smell of coagulated blood, of incinerated bones would haunt her; she would have terrible nightmares in which ghoulish crematoria loomed in the fog. And she would recognise the traces of the intense hatred she'd felt as a child, whenever her father had explained over the dinner table, moving round the plates and forks, how that madman, that criminal had advanced, how he'd entered Russia, how he'd got as far as Stalingrad.

I watched her coming towards me with the cup of coffee in one hand and the sugar bowl in the other. Were we not both kidding each other in our heart of hearts? She must think I'd come all the way from Bogotá to accompany her in her futile ritual. But what I wanted was relief from the tension I could feel mounting inside me, choking me. Yet neither of us could do anything to help the other. She must know perfectly well the ritual was going to get her nowhere; I knew no one could free me from the sensation of failure, of having made a mistake, which always seemed to mar my major stage triumphs. Someone ought to be able to explain why unhappiness homes in on you precisely at those moments when everything seems to be in perfect order; anyway, my son could look after himself, good for him if he's found his ideal place to live, even if it means being a loser.

So, it was time to go. She went over to the dining table littered with papers and put something in her handbag; then she disappeared behind the flowery curtain and brought out an impeccably cut jacket, matching her tartan skirt. (So that was where she hung her clothes…) She took out a white scarf and tied it round her neck. She glanced at me and produced an identical scarf for me.

'I've got a scarf, thanks.'

She stood looking at me.

'That's not the point. It's in case you want to go dressed like the rest of us. We all wear a white scarf as a token.'

I clutched the white scarf and felt close to tears.

'The last time I saw a big demonstration waving white scarves was in Chile, a few months ago, outside La Moneda Palace. It's a wonderful sight to see thousands of white scarves waving in the air.'

'We've got thousands of white scarves too,' she replied as she locked the door. 'But it's not a wonderful sight.'

As we went down the stairs I said it was a sign of hope, anyway. We were met by a disgusting smell of cabbage soup.

'So we believe,' she murmured out on the pavement, pressing my hand. She was smiling ruefully, as if apologising for being less than honest with me.

The two women walk one behind the other because of the narrow pavement and the odd person sitting out on the doorstep with legs protruding, in time-honoured indifference to the passers-by. She would rather have gone down another street, Florida for example, but Elena presumably wanted to avoid the risk of bumping into someone she knew. She looked down the first side-street towards the port, and with a twinge of nostalgia recognised the distant outlines of the ships at anchor. It was as if she'd flashed back to the childhood days when ships and ports dizzied her with an attraction nothing else could equal, rescuing her from the urban greyness of Buenos Aires. They went on walking in silence till they came out into the square.

She stopped short, dazzled by the whiteness of that vast, bleak, open space, with its ludicrous obelisk sticking up in the middle. 'It must be the light reflecting on the paving stones,' she thought, confronted by a stream of images in which she crossed the square again and again, first as a child and then as a girl. She began to make her way falteringly across the horrid square, squinting at the blinding light. When finally she opened her eyes wide, she saw the sun was still high overhead, in an unblemished sky without a hint of cloud. She felt irritated by that conjunction of blue and white, evoking the national colours and flag. Argentine nationalism was, it seemed, doomed to belong to the category of the kitsch. Give her the tropics any day, with their stormy skies perpetually rent by the play of warring elements. She noted that a handful of people, no more than that, were dotted around the middle of the square. But something felt wrong. She looked and looked again, trying to work out what was out of place in that provincial square whose every detail she knew so well. Her eyes went from the Cabildo to the Cathedral, and back again. The Casa Rosada, as unspeakably hideous as ever, was blocking the view of the river. When would they pull that pink monstrosity down? Everything was as it had always been, drab, bare and ugly. And then it hit her; apart from the groups of women arriving for the demonstration, there was nobody in the square. No sightseers were standing around, no school children or men going about their daily business were hurrying across it, no old people were sunning themselves on the park benches. There were no street vendors anywhere to be seen. 'I'm going mad like the other women,' she thought, and looked round the square again, surveying it inch by inch. The gathering in the middle of the square was growing; women on their own or arm-in-arm were streaming out of the side-streets. 'I can't believe it,' she said to herself again. 'Why is there no one here?' She turned round and saw four women coming towards her, knotting their scarves under their chins. On the corner behind them, a little girl was tying her scarf round her neck. She looked up at the windows overlooking the square. No one was looking out. With a puzzled frown, she took her white scarf out of her bag and put it on. Elena was watching the demonstration grow from the pavement at the edge of the square. But her mind was completely taken up with the fact that, at half past four in the afternoon, there was not a single person there except for the women taking part in the demonstration. Elena took Victoria's photograph out of her handbag and started to study it; it looked somewhat the worse for wear, though she did her best to flatten it out and straighten the corners. She felt embarrassed to ask if she could have a look at it. From what she could make out, it seemed that Victoria was standing on a beach though wearing a polo-neck sweater and trousers. Did she have her hands in her pockets? But Elena lowered the photo and started to walk towards the centre of the square. In the fraction of a second that she was left stranded not knowing quite what to do, a woman dashed past with a bundle of duplicated lists and handed her one. It went on for twenty-three pages; she felt an urge to count the names and started to run her forefinger down the columns to work out how many names were on each page. She'd got to the forty-fifth line when someone stopped at her elbow and said: 'You needn't bother to count them, sister, there are about a thousand names down here, but the actual number who've disappeared is much higher than that. We've only just started compiling the lists. The job is complicated by the fact that a lot of people are unwilling to give the full names and ages, or the parents' names and phone numbers.' She shrugged her shoulders and walked on. She felt annoyed with the woman for calling her 'sister' and poking her nose into what was none of her business, but she took another glance at the list. Only now did she notice the ages; they mostly ranged from fifteen to twenty-five; she went on going through it page by page. A woman of sixty-eight, another of seventy-five. She shuddered. A four-month-old baby, a two-year-old girl, another of five, a brother and sister of three and four. The list in her hand began to quiver. How can a four-month-old baby disappear? The entry read: Anselmo Furco, four months, disappeared on... Parents: Juan Gustavo Furco, 23, Alicia, 20, also missing. It was followed by the name, address and telephone number of the grandparents. A violent lurch in the pit of her stomach made her grope for the nearest wall to lean against. Someone came up to her and said: 'Come on now, you mustn't give up.' They steered her back to the square. She felt better in the open air and looked around her. So these were the Madwomen of the Plaza de Mayo ... The number of women was incredible and so was the silence; apart from the rapid footsteps and muffled greetings, there was not a sound. Not a single prison van, not a single policeman, not a single army jeep was in sight. The Casa Rosada looked like a stage set, with thick curtains drawn across its windows. There were no grenadier guards on sentry duty at the gates either. It was the realisation that the grenadier guards were not there that gave her a sudden, terrifying insight into the enemy's machinations: *every Thursday, for the two to three hours during which the demonstration took place, the Plaza de Mayo was wiped off the map*. They couldn't fire on the women or lock them all up. It would have undermined the concerted effort they'd made to project a carefree image of 'the Argentina I love'. Their ploy was simply to ignore them; to ignore the existence of the square and of the madwomen stamping their feet. Had they arrived at that degree of sophistication? And why not, if the same sophistication operated at the level of tortures and abductions? A developed nation does things properly.

She was beginning to give way to despair; more questions flooded into her head. What about the people who regularly passed through the square at that time of day? What about the bank clerks? What about the crowds permanently gathered on the corner by the Cabildo? Where the devil were they? What about the priests and parishioners who every afternoon without fail went to pray in the Cathedral? Did they sneak out of the back door or stay waiting inside in the dark? What about the people who at that precise moment had to get an important document signed at the solicitor's offices bordering the square? How had they managed to get such a motley collection of people, who couldn't possibly have come to a joint agreement, to melt into thin air? What had provoked this reaction of blind terror in each and every one of them? Or were they unanimously shunning this vast array of desperate women because it brought them face to face with a grief that words could not convey? And the same cowards who would not risk setting an immaculately shod foot in the square would loudly proclaim, contented citizens all, that they were avid football fans, that they ate meat every day, that they holidayed at Mar del Plata whenever the fancy took them, that they wouldn't dream of missing a Sunday on the beach despite all those dreadful rumours — put around by the enemies of the fatherland — of bodies floating in the River Plate. Or did they sleep uneasily at night?

Meanwhile more and more women kept on arriving; by now the square was so packed they were spilling out into the roadway. She lost sight of Elena and knew there was no point trying to look for her in such a crowd, but she plunged into it all the same, edging her way forward as best she could.

'Did I tell you I've got some terrible photos a friend took there one Thursday? If I'd known we were going to talk about it I'd have brought them with me. To be honest, I never really understood why you went back to Buenos Aires. Anyway, you wouldn't want to look at my pictures if you saw it for yourself. There's another group here that's printing copies of all the photographs in their records. That's an even more gruesome sight. But the photos of the missing children are important, because they've been known to turn up in other countries. It's a kind of hell we're living in.'

And what a hell, Dolores! A new man-made version, such as no one ever imagined. Without a word or command being uttered, the women raised the photographs above their heads. Why, when there was no one there to see them? I expected that, with so much handling and fondling, those childlike faces would soon be disfigured past the point of recognition. Near me, an old woman was holding up a cheap studio portrait with both hands. The girl was smiling stiffly, her head tilted to one side, no doubt obeying the photographer's instructions. She was sitting with her legs crossed, an organdie dress covering her knees. Another woman was holding a passport photograph in the palm of her hand, shielding it as if it were an egg she'd just that minute hatched; she raised it gingerly and started to wave it from side to side; she couldn't stop shaking and the tears were streaming down her face, but she kept her lips tightly pressed together. A woman right next to me took out of her handbag a tiny picture in an oval frame. She looked at me and smiled apologetically. The only photos she had of him were taken when he was a child, if only she'd known... I asked her how old he was now. 'He'll be twenty next month. We were so proud of him. We were going to hold a party to celebrate.' She could barely finish the sentence, but she pulled herself together, sighed and raised the tiny frame as high as she could, along with all the other photographs. I started to feel uncomfortable just standing there with nothing to hold up. I raised the list with both hands and waited expectantly. Was that it? Just this coming together to share one's silent grief with the silent grief of others?

And that was when it started, Dolores, I can't explain to you what it was that happened. How can I find the words? I could say that suddenly someone started to shout and everyone started shouting and in a matter of minutes the whole square was one single shout. But that wouldn't begin to tell you what it was like. There are so many people shouting all over the place... And you'll probably smile if I tell you I started to shout as well, though it had nothing to do with me, and I've no idea what I shouted, I couldn't understand a word of what the other women were shouting either, because it was as if the words were severed from one another by the sobbing and howling. Every now and then I thought I heard the words 'Where are they?', 'Where are they?' but it may have been my imagination. And yet they must have been voicing some demand that served as a focus for the general mood of anger, because the crowd of women surged forward like a tide. They continued to advance, we knocked into one another, stumbling over each other's feet. The chaos was indescribable as hundreds of sheets of paper were tossed into the air. I did exactly the same as the madwomen, and I couldn't begin to tell you what I felt; it was as if someone was trying to rip my insides out and I was clinging on to them for all I was worth. But that's not it, either. I can't be sure it was really like that. I keep groping for the words but it's useless. I heard an alarming whirring sound overhead and ducked instinctively; it soon dawned on me it was the pigeons flapping their wings in terror as they flew round and round, not knowing where to settle. They went on wheeling frantically, feathers flurrying, beaks snapping furiously. I collided head-on with a girl who was groaning, she can't have been more than twenty. Who had she lost? Her baby, her husband, her parents? I couldn't see the crumpled photo she was clutching with both hands. I thought I glimpsed a snatch of Elena's jacket in the middle of a circle of women and I elbowed my way towards her. She was part of a chorus chanting in unison, and this time I could clearly hear the words 'Where are they?', 'Where are they?' She had her back to me, but she didn't turn round even when I put my hand on her shoulder and shook her. Then I shouted her name. You say you knew her well, Dolores, but at that moment you'd never have recognised her. I'd grown up with her but she was a complete stranger to me. I wish I could forget that twisted face, that gaping, howling mouth and, even worse, her skin, that delicate skin of hers, discoloured with purple blotches. She wasn't holding Victoria's photo up in the air but was clasping it to her chest with both hands, huddling over it; an old woman cowering in the face of death. I put my arm round her and started to chant with her. Until everything began to quieten down. The madwomen began to drift away. Three women of indeterminate age were trying to calm another woman who was shaking her clenched fist at the Casa Rosada. They started to straighten their jackets, smooth their blouses, resettle their handbags on their arms; they tidied their hair and looked around for the best way out of the square. The crowd thinned out, revealing the paving stones strewn with stencilled sheets. I felt completely stunned, I needed more time to recover. I lost sight of Elena again. It was only a matter of minutes before the square had emptied

90

itself. A woman took a packet out of her bag and started to throw bits of bread to the pigeons, but they were still chary; they kept skidding on the bits of paper and taking off again in panic, leaving the food. I felt like kicking the pigeons, but I took pity on the woman; how many times had she come to feed them with her missing son or daughter?

I crossed over to the opposite pavement and, looking up at the sky, saw that the pigeons were reassembling in flying formation and winging their way back to their usual perch on the obelisk. My friend was waiting for me on the corner of the Calle San Martín; her pale pointed face was calm and serene.

She must have noticed something alarming in my expression, because she gaped at me as if about to say something. Then she shook her head. 'Don't let it upset you like that, don't let it upset you like that,' she murmured and now it was her turn to put her arm round me. But I did something awful, really awful, I'll never forgive myself for it.

'What did you do?' the girl asked, putting down the blazer she was about to put on.

'I broke away from her and ran out into the middle of the road shouting how was I supposed to feel, for Christ's sake, how was I supposed to feel, and why didn't those bastards hiding behind the curtains come out into the open; I was ranting and raving like a maniac, while she stood there going red as if I'd slapped her in the face.'

Dolores sat watching her cigarette go out in the ashtray.

'I created a real scandal. And do you think anyone came out to see what was going on, do you think anyone looked out of the window? Not a soul.'

'I'm sorry,' Elena said. 'I'm really sorry.'

But I wasn't sorry; what I was feeling was completely different, horribly different. I told Elena I was going back to the square. She glanced at me briefly without a word, then turned on her heels and went back home, presumably. The square was still empty, or almost empty, I don't remember exactly. I sat down on a bench, muttering 'How am I sup-

posed to feel, for Christ's sake, how am I supposed to feel?'
over and over again, till I'd said it so many times it started
to lose its force. I was distracted by the sight of an old man
doing his utmost to get a little boy he was holding by the
hand to touch a pigeon. I looked around me and realised why
I'd returned to the square, I'd returned to watch the rats slink-
ing back once they'd sensed that danger was over. Now the
whole square was full of rats loitering or scurrying around.
More and more rats kept pouring in and out of the side-streets.
I looked over at the Cathedral and saw the steps lined with
rats. But were they really rats? Disgusting, stinking, cowardly
rats? Ought they to be exterminated like vermin? I looked
at the little boy chasing the pigeons. I looked at the Casa
Rosada, two grenadier guards were on sentry duty. At that
point I leant my head against the back of the iron bench and
began to weep, silently, so no one would notice.

The girl put her blazer on and went to look out of the window.
  'It's got dark,' she said. 'The last thing I wanted was to
go home in the dark.'
  But something else was obviously on her mind. As they
turned to face each other at the front door, she clutched her
by the arm.
  'I don't know how one's supposed to feel about it either.
All I know is that you have to find some kind of breathing
space. Because if you don't have room to breathe, you'll be
dead as well. And the worst of it isn't that you'll be dead
but that you'll have added another corpse to their collection.'

She looked at her watch but instantly wished she hadn't. She'd probably interpret it as an unfriendly gesture, especially when she'd been so touchy all afternoon. 'Now we'll get into a conversation about how late the bus is,' she thought apprehensively.

As if to order, the woman said, 'It's a lousy service.' And added, 'You're lucky if they come once in a blue moon.'

Both were standing on the edge of the pavement. The last, residual light of evening, sensuous and shimmering, hovered between the trees.

'It ought to be warmer at this time of year, don't you think?'

'But it's not cold,' the older woman replied almost defensively. 'The problem is the wind. It's always windy here.'

'How far are you from the beach?'

'About ten or twelve blocks away.' She was about to go on, but stopped.

The girl was staring up at the sky.

'I've only just noticed they've cut back the eucalyptus trees. The philistines.'

'They insist the roots undermine the foundations of the houses and that they could blow down in the wind. One tree over there did come crashing down, bringing half a roof with it. But I agree they're philistines. Do you remember how beautiful this avenue used to be?'

Now both of them were craning their necks, looking up at the sky. Then they both turned to peer down the road. No sign of the bus. The street had formerly been the driveway to an estate, lined with tall, arching trees; with the tree trunks

cut back, it looked forlorn. To make things worse, tiny branches were sprouting from the sawn-off stumps. How many
years would it take them to grow into billowing trees again?
The houses, separated by plots of uncultivated land, could
no longer hide their starkness. The gardens were not fenced
off and the whole area looked like a wilderness. 'It's either
a wealthy district or else it's a wasteland,' the girl thought
vaguely. 'Everything in Montevideo is turning into a
wasteland.'

'It's like being in the country here,' she said for the sake
of saying something. The words sounded lame, for she hated
the countryside and the endless expanse of dreary, run-down
ranches encircling the city. But the other woman seemed to
like it precisely for that reason. Except that she would have
liked to be closer to the beach and the old casino, which she
loved. She was intrigued by that empty shell of a building,
with its deserted terraces and boarded-up saloons.

The girl made an effort to imagine why someone might
find such an eyesore intriguing but couldn't.

'How long has it been empty?' the woman asked.

'I don't really know. For ages, because it closed down
when my parents were still quite young. My mother is always
going on about how she spent her honeymoon there.'

'Really?' she exclaimed. 'But it must have been a luxury
hotel!'

She felt embarrassed, realising she found the idea
incongruous. How could her mother have got enough money
together to stay at a hotel like that? She felt it would be rude
to ask. Anyway, what did it matter to her whether her mother
had or hadn't been able to afford it?

'It was a luxury hotel,' the girl muttered sullenly. 'But my
mother won a free week's stay there as a prize for being the
most efficient teacher at school, or something like that.'

She stopped short. it was a fact that her mother had stayed
there, too bad if she didn't believe her. Despite her mother's
idyllic memories of her stay, which she embellished pro-
gressively over the years, she must have had a lousy time

in that luxury hotel, with her coat shiny with wear, not knowing how to summon the waiters. She found the idea of her mother ever having been young grotesque, if not obscene; even more so the thought of her having had a honeymoon. What a stupid name for something more like a rape! No doubt it was as a result of that wretched stay in the hotel, peeking out through the Venetian blinds, scared to go out on the terraces or into the saloons, that she was here now waiting for the bus like an idiot. Twenty-eight lousy years of existence, some favour they'd done her bringing her into this world! She calculated that she was seven years older than the boy missing in the chaos in Santiago. Irene could be her mother. She studied her as she went out into the middle of the road to see if the bus was coming. She was visibly overwrought and on the verge of breakdown; a mere shadow of the compelling, outrageous actress, with her long, scarlet stockings, she'd been five years ago. To be fair, everyone was a mere shadow of his or her former self (with the possible exception of Luisa, looking after her Siamese cats in Lyons). She felt a certain relish at the thought that Irene was more fragile than her public image would have led her to expect, and that if her son disappeared without trace, she would fall to pieces completely. Some people manage to pick themselves up off the ground, others stay flattened for ever; after what she'd been through, everyone fell into one or other of those categories as far as she was concerned. No, Irene will never get over it. Or will she manage to keep up her pretence of eternal youth? She was always putting on an act for someone; hadn't she just got herself a high-powered husband? And she no doubt still had her following of devotees and admirers. But how else could she be expected to behave if she had a natural gift for seduction? She recalled the passionate response she'd produced in her when they first met, she'd not wanted to leave her side for a single second. Had she been wrong to think she was open to any new experience, given a bit of persuasion? But what could the inexperienced, provincial girl she'd been five years ago have offered her? A budding writer, a weak student, a nonentity; forget it. And yet the actress had accepted her devotion; had chosen to spend her time with them, a band of hapless revolutionaries, rather than with the friends she must have had in Montevideo as everywhere else; she'd listened to her and understood her. She could have revealed who she was at that awful moment when they were dragged off to prison from Luisa's house, but she'd chosen not to. Had it been a game for her, had she really been interested in her or was it just a pretence? Her attraction lay precisely in the inexplicability of her behaviour. Being with her made you feel like a disconcerted sailor who, after a long and stormy crossing, suddenly catches sight of the longed-for haven. Nothing was quite like being with her, nothing in the world.

She closed her eyes. Don't say she was going to let herself slip back into that obsessive devotion! Why not, after all? Even in her present state of anguish about what was happening in Chile, her despair at the lack of news, hadn't she still comforted her with her well-intentioned illusions? How many times that afternoon had she shown obvious signs of distress at all she'd gone through? And it wasn't just pity, but joy at being alive in spite of everything. For years she'd refused to let herself think about Enrique or the baby (a little girl, the nurse had said) they'd made her miscarry by stamping on her belly. But today she had thought about them and had talked openly about Enrique, with a tangible, clearcut pain that in a way had done her good. Only the intensity of being with her could have worked such a miracle. She hadn't said so in so many words, but she'd made her see clearly for the first time that this jumble of blood and horror and teeth and claws was part of her life, something she had to accept as part of herself; and that the unfeeling salvation she'd been clutching at desperately would be meaningless if she pretended that the unspeakable suffering she'd experienced had never happened. It wasn't a question of Christian expiation, she must be careful not to fall into that trap, but a matter of accepting that what has happened to you, for good or for ill, is part of you, and that it can be a very important part. If you are able to assimilate it. If you are able to be clear about what it means. Wasn't that what she ought to be writing about? She was amazed to find such ideas occurring to her, and to discover that she and the things that were part of her, the scraps of paper she systematically covered with lines of verse, her dreary existence, had a place in this world.

Her arms folded tightly across her chest to protect herself from the icy wind, Irene was smiling at her from the middle of the road.

What was she smiling at? What would happen if right now, the phone rang and she ran indoors and they told her? How can a smile be such an integral part of a face? She was beset by unkind thoughts, which she couldn't suppress. 'It must be because I'm jealous,' she thought, 'because I hardly ever smile, I've forgotten how to.' It had amused her to see her surrounded by all those fetishes, those revolting wood carvings she fondled so lovingly and all the useless objects she no doubt carted around with her wherever she went. She found it ironic that her cosmopolitan agnosticism, so typical of Buenos Aires, should have been irremediably eroded by her travels and long periods spent living in the Caribbean. She might smile apologetically, insisting she was completely non-religious, but there, all around her, were the voodoo figures.

'I think there's one coming,' she heard her say. She was hopping from one foot to the other and in the growing darkness could have passed for a schoolgirl.

She found it hard to drag herself out of her thoughts. Something inside her didn't want to leave. She wanted to know what would happen after the woman had gently closed the front door behind her. Would she collapse in a heap? Would she moan and groan, doubled up on the tiled floor? Would she bury her head in her hands waiting for the phone to ring? Or would she light up a cigarette and absent-mindedly stroke the misshapen wooden heads?

'Keep in touch this time,' her warm voice was saying. She

desperately wanted to stay enveloped by the sound of that voice. Again she felt a violent need to go on being with her, what was the matter with her? She heard herself reply: 'I'll keep in touch, I promise, but make sure you contact me if you get some news.'

'Wait, you haven't told me where you're living now. Do your parents still live in the same place? Is that the best place to ring you?'

The girl rummaged in her bag for a piece of paper and clumsily scribbled a number. No, she didn't live at home any more, she hadn't for some time. Now she was renting a room. The family in the boarding house were okay, they kept out of her way.

'I'll ring you without fail,' she said, taking the scrap of paper.

The bus was almost at the stop and the girl felt an urgent need for her to say something, anything, just to hear her voice.

'It takes an incredibly roundabout route to the centre,' she said in a playful tone, as if reading her thoughts. 'You'll have time to write a book on the way. Have you got enough paper to keep you going?'

'No, how careless of me,' Dolores replied in like fashion. 'I'll do my best to memorise it in my head.'

The woman laughed, clasped her by the shoulders and gave her an affectionate shake. Her fingers were gentle but surprisingly firm.

'Take care,' they both said at the same time, and the elder woman tossed her head back laughing.

'Come on now, ladies,' the driver muttered vaguely, giving them a sideways look.

Dolores jumped inside. She looked back and saw her still standing by the side of the road. The wind was blowing her hair across her face.

It was the beginning of the route and the bus was almost empty. The only passenger was an old man sitting at the back, staring fixedly out of the window.

The girl took a seat near the driver. He was humming a tune, and the bus crawled up the hill towards the big gateway. He took out from under his seat a gourd and pipe for sipping maté, and slowly poured some water from a thermos, his elbow on the steering wheel. 'This country is going to the dogs,' she thought, and was immediately cross with herself for reacting so indignantly. Why shouldn't the poor bloke drink his maté, after all? Was anyone in a hurry? There was no one around and nothing to do in Montevideo these days. It made no difference whether you went out or stayed at home, whether you were alive or dead. The bus remained empty until, after several stops, a woman got on trailing a little boy behind her. As she got on, the driver put his maté and thermos away under his seat and for a minute looked as though he was about to start driving in earnest, but then began to whistle under his breath, still crawling along at a snail's pace.

They were going through a vast expanse of uncultivated land, with a few houses dotted about in the dark. The sky was now completely black; she shielded her eyes with her hand to see more clearly, but decided the dreariness of the outside world would only make her feel angry and, with a sigh, went back to staring at the grubby floor. The bus braked and stopped on a corner for another passenger to get on. Outside was a café, through whose windows you could see a pool table with several men playing in silence. The low ceiling light lit up a murky round patch in the middle of the table. 'It ought to be green,' she thought with an unwarranted anxiety. The men were cut in two by the lampshade. One leant forward making ready to play, and his face came into the circle of light. He had a dead fag-end sticking out of the corner of his mouth. She was struck by the ugliness of the peeling café walls.

She closed her eyes. What would happen if she started to pray and begged and begged someone or something to make Victoria appear in front of her, looking just the way she had the last time she'd seen her? It would be enough to see her again just once, just once I beg of you. But the sight of the man's furrowed brow as he chewed his fag-end and aimed his cue at the ball made it impossible for her to concentrate on her prayer. She'd never had much luck with prayers, probably because she didn't believe in them and knew perfectly well there was no one to pray to.

She was glad she hadn't let a word out all afternoon about her friendship with Victoria. What was the point? It was better for Irene to go on believing she was just another misguided upper-class girl, mindlessly playing at revolution because she'd run out of new toys. But it was unfair of her to attribute such thoughts to Irene. It was pretty clear from their conversation that not only did she understand Victoria but that she also sympathised with her; otherwise she wouldn't have told her about the letter she'd received from her in Bogotá. Wasn't that precisely what irritated her, that Irene should feel such sympathy for Victoria? Because that called into question all her resentment towards her parents and her belief, gained from bitter experience, that the older generation had no understanding of young people. At least her parents didn't; nor did Enrique's mother. So when they took your side you had good reason to be suspicious; there was always some unconfessed motive, usually of an emotional order. The urge for possession, first and foremost.

Irene thinking my son, my beloved son who is mine alone and must go on being mine alone and no one can take him from me; and Victoria's mother going on about my precious daughter who they dragged away from my penthouse with its view over the river and whose existence they dare to deny as if I'd never given birth to her, nursed her, brought her up, taught her good table manners. In the end it always boiled down to a matter of private property. Didn't her own mother spend the whole day moping indoors because they did this, that and the other to her darling daughter? And hadn't her father renounced the coffee he'd sipped for forty-three years at the same table in the same bar on the same corner, and quarrelled with his colleagues at the office to boot, all because someone had talked in a loud voice about those long-haired drop-outs who deserved to be exterminated like rats? When of course he felt just the same about long-haired drop-outs... But she, like Victoria, was the private property of a family who, all because of what she'd done, could no longer raise their heads in the street; and yet they wouldn't let go of her either. The complaints she'd had to sit through when she decided to move out to a rented room so they'd leave her in peace for once in her life, informing them of the fact in no uncertain terms to bring it home to them that her reason for leaving was that she couldn't take their moaning any more. And didn't Enrique's mother, two years after it all, still keep coming to see her, dressed in mourning like a crow but tough, energetic and unrelenting, because although the brutes told me he was dead and gave me the sealed coffin with strict orders not to open it (you never know in such cases what pieces you're likely to find or what pieces are likely to be missing), the fact is I never actually saw my son, my poor little Quique, and who knows... She'd finally stopped saying 'Quique', if only because she noticed the unmistakable look of hatred on her daughter-in-law's face; but she kept on coming to see her and would sit there talking about her Enrique, and how in the street she'd bumped into some of her Enrique's schoolfriends whom she hadn't seen for years, and how all of them, to a man, were against this bunch of murderers. She would utter the word 'murderers' coyly, without a trace of anger, as if it had slipped out by mistake. When it was a word that ought to be shouted, spat out, spluttered; how could you simply say it?

Utter-splutter-utter-splutter; she toyed with the words; the jogging of the bus was making her feel drowsy but she didn't want to lose track of her thoughts. Where was she? That's right, mothers, the usual loathsome, dreaded topic. And yet she'd no right to complain. She took pleasure in recalling Irene's ageing face, the unkind marks left by the years, her unmistakable anxiety. Another one who refused to give up. Was she different from the others or would she too fight tooth and nail to defend her right to her son as a piece of personal property? Who was she trying to save? Herself or her son? But she had to think this through properly. She was bound to admit, however reluctantly, that she knew a lot of mothers who'd behaved magnificently over the past few terrible years. And wasn't that precisely what annoyed her? Would she respect those mothers more if they renounced their children? It would be more logical. For what right did they, as young people, have to risk their lives when those same lives had been carefully wadded with all those hard-earned banknotes, insurance policies, shares, superannuation schemes amassed over a lifetime of forced labour? For example, why didn't her father insult her because he'd had to give up the cups of coffee and games of pool with his friends that were the only pleasures he had in life? Why had her mother broken with the Salto Schoolteachers' Association, whose monthly meetings she'd attended regularly till this chain of disasters had struck? Why didn't they fling it in her face openly, disown her, curse her, instead of merely retracting their tentacles like an octopus? They hadn't punished her for what she'd done, but weighed her down with an ever-increasing burden of guilt for the fact that her mother was always snivelling behind the door, never coming into the room and never going to sit outside the front door, in her housecoat, as she always used to do in summer, and for the fact that her father, in his pyjamas, perspiring in the stifling heat indoors, would sink into a glum silence pretending to read the paper. But he wasn't reading it, she was perfectly aware of that; he was thinking about her; always forever thinking about her and what had happened to her.

And the anger built up inside her until one day she decided to leave, to rid herself of the intolerable burden of guilt.

Then there was Victoria's mother. She'd got to know Elena as well as if she'd lived in her house or slept in her bed, though she hadn't said a word about it during the whole afternoon. The less said, the better. The habit of not talking without permission from the group leader, which had become second nature to her and could not be broken.

She'd argued with Victoria when she was instructed first to follow Elena and later to accompany her, so she would have a good alibi if she were interrogated. She'd loathed all that wandering up and down the Calle Sante Fe, looking round the boutiques, having tea in the packed tea rooms, listening to tedious lectures in half-empty halls. To make things worse, events proved her right. What brute in uniform cared a damn about whether or not she had a good alibi? Once again she was struck by the absurdity of the fact that, such a short time ago, they'd still believed in verdicts, judges, indictments, trials, laws. What legal system, what defunct, non-existent Argentina were they thinking of? And even after taking over as leader of the group, after Andrés had been shot down, Victoria continued to think that the battle was being fought in the country they'd been taught to believe in at school; only towards the end was she known to admit, somewhat sceptically, that they might all end up being massacred in cold blood.

Victoria joined the movement shortly after the massacre at Trelew. No one understood why she'd taken what appeared to be a sudden decision, that seemed out of keeping with the apparent unease she'd always displayed with her more radical fellow-students. Or perhaps it was before and not after. She recalls how Andrés, speaking of that devastatingly beautiful girl, had told her she'd taken to skipping lectures. In fact she would disappear for several weeks at a time, which could not fail to be noticed since she was the kind of person who inevitably attracted attention. When she reappeared after her absences, she would join the students endlessly debating in the university café, listening attentively to the arguments of all and sundry but hardly ever putting in a word. Which is probably why she appealed to Andrés, who hated show-offs and bossy women. On the odd occasion when she made a contribution to the debate, she would immediately retreat and blush on seeing everyone fall silent and turn to look at her. The times they met in the penthouse to talk about exams or the group projects they had to do at university, her fellow students discovered, not without sarcastic comment, how at ease she was with the opulent furniture and Persian carpets, remaining unaffected by their jokes about the maids with lace aprons or the English silver tea service. She would merely reply with a disarming smile, not saying a word. As for Elena, on such occasions she would put in a discreet appearance, giving everyone a welcoming nod and asking if they had everything they needed. Inhibited, they would reply yes, they were fine thanks. The only one who would get up to greet her and shake hands was Andrés, whereupon Elena would put on her most charming smile, while casting a disapproving look at the worn jeans and baggy sweater disfiguring her daughter. And yet Victoria's good looks were so self-evident nothing could detract from them. Her attractiveness lay partly in her exceptionally thick golden hair, which cascaded out of the rubber band holding it back; or perhaps in the brilliance of her grass-green eyes, an unreal poster-paint green, which she usually kept half closed and which, when they flashed open, would suddenly light up a face as if out of a Florentine drawing, disconcertingly modified by the broad, sweeping, modern brushstroke of her mouth.

They started to take her seriously when she took to joining them in the café, listening silently to their discussions, but she remained the heiress to a scandalously wealthy Argentinian family, a perfect example of bourgeois complacency. As a result, the legend of Victoria's beauty, self-centredness and indifference died hard, despite her efforts to live it down.

As to be expected, Andrés was the one least taken in by inauspicious appearances. Victoria opened up with him as with no one else. She even went so far as to tell him she'd had a major row with her father when she'd flatly refused to finish her studies in Europe or the States, which was what her father had in mind for her. Andrés asked her why she didn't want to go abroad. The reply was an obvious one, but it was typical of her straightforward manner; she felt at home in Argentina, she was interested in her subject, she intended to make her career in Buenos Aires; so why go abroad? Andrés wondered for a moment whether a boyfriend was involved, but he knew her relations with her fellow students were distant if not aloof. A shy girl, who he'd like to win over to the cause precisely because there was nothing devious about her, because she did everything thoroughly and on time, always complying with what was expected of her. But at the same time her shyness was inhibiting even for a born leader like Andrés. He left things for a later occasion. They had all the time in the world.

The conversation really churned things up inside me. How long has it been since I last thought of Luisa, for example? Even when I heard she'd left for Lyons I didn't think about her all that much. And now Luisa emerges as a key figure in this woeful story. It was precisely as a consequence of the night they arrested us all at her house that the visits to Buenos Aires started and I made contact with Andrés' group. I made the first trip almost immediately after my release, just a week after being locked up in solitary confinement, hearing nothing but the occasional scream and the thuds that inevitably accompanied the interrogation sessions. I lost my fear of prison and the police, even though we failed to secure Enrique or Juan's release, despite kicking up a tremendous fuss. (And Luisa did more than anyone.) One day, when I got to the prison for the routine visit, I was told Enrique had been transferred. No one could tell me where to. All the lawyers in the world, all Luisa's furious protests to her influential friends were to no avail. But I don't want to think about Enrique; I'm losing track of what happened when; it makes me break out into a sweat just to think of the phone call announcing the delivery of the sealed coffin. When was it that they arrested me for the second time? Was it before that or after? When did the fear start, the anguish? Oh no, dear God, please, please, no.

I didn't enjoy my first trip to Buenos Aires much. I was a bit suspicious of the Argentinian students' brash manner, and I bungled a lot of things out of fear that they'd treat me like an inexperienced provincial. They were not particularly open with me and only a long time afterwards did Andrés tell me, with a smile, that he'd found me an insufferable Uruguayan pedant; the result of the misunderstandings and reticence on both sides was that I didn't have much to report to my group when I got back to Montevideo. But I was well aware of the strategic importance of our operating together. They had more funds than us and, above all, more people. We didn't have the wherewithall to replace anyone who was taken prisoner or killed. (Which was happening more and more.) They replaced people straightaway and seemed invincible. The frequency of my trips to Buenos Aires increased, I got to know Andrés and his group better and my views changed radically. I've never known anyone who had such an ability to give meaning to his acts as Andrés. He loathed and feared improvisation and emotional outbursts on the part of members of the group. He, like Victoria, came from an upper-class Argentinian family, but precisely for that reason was wary of other young people from the same class. Unlike the others, he acted like an experienced politician who had a complete grasp of the situation and regards it as vital to have grassroots support. His confidants were two boys from the slums, both trade unionists, which put a lot of people's backs up. But no one dared challenge him. And to think that he's dead, I can't bear it . . . Andrés always believed in the inevitability of victory. It was just a matter of time, discipline and effort; no impatience, please. Death didn't enter into his calculations; it was a possibility, for sure, but a remote one, dependent on how well thought out one's actions were. The new recruits used to say that, with Andrés, passing the admission test was tough; but he firmly believed that the movement would fall to pieces if it admitted every half-crazy kid bent on becoming a revolutionary after having a punch-up with daddy for refusing to buy him a car. No doubt he was exaggerating, but the fact is, the only criterion he took into account was the applicant's ideological soundness. Speaking of fathers, Andrés was the most devoted son I've ever met. You could see him positively puff up with pride when talking of his father, an old liberal lawyer. Andrés lived on his own, but father and son spent a lot of time together. And it had to be his poor father who . . .

It's not Andrés but Victoria who concerns me. Her presence is overpowering. It leaves no room for thoughts of anyone else. Everyone was surprised when she joined the group; a lot of us thought her only forte was the tea with scones on a silver tray. When I got to Buenos Aires a few days after she'd been admitted, people were still making cryptic comments, but no one dared contradict Andrés. And she also inhibited criticism, with her irresistible, disarming smile. But, come to think of it, Victoria wasn't smiling much at the time, if at all. She was pale and drawn but, oddly, the qualities that previously had been barely visible now came to the fore. We started to see each other more and more because the need for coordination between the fronts in both countries was becoming desperately urgent.

Dolores ended up getting on better with the Argentinians than with her Uruguayan comrades. Her group in Montevideo, left decimated by the raid on Luisa's house, fell to pieces. They finally released Néstor and Flaquita, who vanished without trace and didn't want to know about armed struggle; but four of their best people stayed inside.

It's all jumbled up in my head, Enrique's death, Juan's broken body, the others who've disappeared. What happened when? How? I've got to sort it out one thing at a time; or else forget it, suppress it, bury it, bury the dead and the living. Their places were taken by young kids, undisciplined and inexperienced. One of them got killed almost instantly in an operation he'd embarked on of his own accord, without consulting anybody. Seventeen years old. Andrés was very worried by the increasing lack of organisation among the groups in Montevideo and, as a result, I went up in his esteem. He would confide in me about everything that was going on, except his motives in admitting Victoria. Then the massacre occurred and everything took on a new dimension. Trelew put an end to any belief in the possibility of a clean fight. Andrés left his apartment and, with his father's help, moved from place to place till things quietened down. He spent ten days in hiding, his only contact with the outside world his father, who would follow him around, confident of finding him. The conversations they had became more and more gloomy, but also brought them closer together. His father would have liked to share Andrés' belief in all-out victory, but was increasingly worried by the risk to his son's life. Andrés would talk in terms of a liberation struggle, but what his father saw in his mind's eye was a program of extermination. He would go home and shut himself up in his study, with a grim look on his face, without saying a word to his wife or other children, despite the fact that they were all passionately concerned to know the latest news about Andrés. Locked in his study, he would review the various possible outcomes, unable to find one that was acceptable; faced with such bleak prospects, his devotion for Andrés and his resolve to stand by him to the last grew stronger and stronger.

When Andrés got back to his apartment, he found three hand-written notes from Victoria under the door. What did she want of him at a time like this? He tore them up and forgot about them. The ensuing period was one of constant alerts, dangerous operations, internal re-organisation, discussion of tactics. It was almost a month before he reappeared at lectures. In his locker he found another folded sheet of mauve writing paper with a message from Victoria. He asked his fellow students if they'd seen her, but no one had. He decided he would have to deal with whatever the problem was. The note gave an address in the Calle San Martín, where she'd be waiting for him whenever he could make it.

Somewhat warily, he went into an old house divided up into rented rooms from the attic downwards. Victoria's note had said 'the floor above FOTO-RAP'. He went up another flight of stairs and knocked unenthusiastically at a door with peeling paint.

As soon as Victoria opened the door, he realised something was seriously wrong. Her magnetic attraction was still there, but something in her had snapped. What had happened? Looking at her and looking around him at the room, he was completely nonplussed. What on earth was she doing in a place like this? But she seemed unaffected by his curiosity and after saying hello and letting him in, without even stopping to offer him a seat, came straight to the point.

I've been looking for you everywhere, please forgive me for being so insistent. I know what things must have been like for you these last few days. But I need help and you're the only person I dare ask.'

The words came rushing out, as if she'd been rehearsing them. When she got to the end she seemed to waver, but regained her composure. He was staring at her, speechless. They were standing in the middle of a dingy studio, covered from top to bottom with notices and posters. It looked uninhabited.

'There are two favours I want to ask of you. First, how to find a doctor to get an abortion. I'm pregnant and I can't have the child now.'

Andrés was utterly at a loss for words. That was the last thing he'd been expecting and his immediate reaction was one of anger. What the hell did he care about her personal problems? But something made him hold his tongue. Why had she said 'now'? Looking at her again, he recognised that the unfamiliar expression on her face was one of fragility and of strength.

'Secondly,' she went on, 'I want you to let me join the

movement. I know my political education is nil and I know exactly what your views on that are. But I think you also know I'm a hard worker.' She'd begun to speak in a confident tone, but by the end her voice had dropped to a near whimper.

'You won't regret it, I promise.'

'Hold on a minute,' Andrés said. He sat down on a chair, but she stayed standing in front of him. He took another look at her. Her hands were in her trouser pockets and she was staring fixedly at a point on the wall.

'Let me ask you a question,' Andrés said slowly and deliberately. 'Or perhaps two questions. The first thing I want to know is whether the two things are related.'

'What do you mean?' she asked, blushing intensely. But she looked him in the eye and murmured 'Yes' in a barely audible whisper.

'The second thing I want to know is why you turned to me, of all people, to get you an abortion.'

Victoria stayed silent for a while. 'Don't say she's going to cry,' he thought apprehensively. She seemed to be making a tremendous effort to hold back the tears.

'Well, never mind if . . .' he started to mutter, but Victoria pulled herself together and took a hand out of her pocket as if to stop him going any further.

'It's all right, let me answer your question. It's just that we often used to joke about how you'd be the baby's godfather. And also because I know you're the only person who won't say a word to anyone.'

Andrés was thrown again. So what had been going on? Who was the father? Don't say he was going to let his emotions get the better of him, when he was the one who was always talking about the need to keep emotions out of it. How long was it since he'd renounced the idea of any kind of private life? No, he mustn't give way to pity. The thing was to find an effective solution. 'You can count on me,' he said to Victoria, looking at the ground. He realised his fists were clenched in his pockets. He took the mauve sheet of writing paper out of one pocket, and held it out to her. 'Give me a note of your phone number.' He looked around him: 'Has this barn got a phone?' He'd managed to regain his usual neutral, ironic tone of voice.

'Of course it has,' she said, rising to the occasion and managing a smile. 'And it's not a barn, it's a studio; it belongs to a couple who left for France. They kept the husband with a hood over his head for a week and then let him go.'

Andrés surveyed the room more carefully. A ladder led up to a raised platform. 'That must be where they made love,' Andrés thought. He tried to get the thought out of his head but couldn't. With who, with which of my friends? It must have been a close friend for him to want me to be the god-father. And what's happened to him? In prison, dead, or missing? It was obvious that the girl was alone and was going through a terrible time.

Victoria handed him back the mauve sheet of paper with the phone number. Her eyes were half closed. 'If she opens them,' Andrés thought, 'the tears will come pouring out.' He went up to her and gave her a quick kiss on the cheek, without putting his arms round her. 'I'll get all the information and ring you as soon as I can.' He left abruptly and ran down the stairs two at a time. Out on the pavement he hesitated for a moment, oblivious to the seedy surroundings. For the first time in years, he felt like going into a bar and getting drunk. He calculated that the bar opposite would be empty at this time of day, that it would be suitably dark inside and that, in his current state of abstinence, four glasses would be enough to make the impossible possible and bring back all the things he'd relegated to the past. Sex and love, happiness, lust; Jesus, what a lifeless, impotent freak he'd become! An empty taxi slowed down and hooted at him. He hailed it and leapt inside. Brusquely he gave the address of his apartment. He reflected that he had at least three meetings to get through in what was left of the day. There was going to be trouble with . . . He shut his eyes and pressed his hand against his forehead. This bitter pill had become his life.

'If it stops for someone to get on at the next stop,' Dolores thought peering out into the dark outside, 'I might catch a glimpse of the house. If there's a light at any of the windows. With any luck...' She recognised the cornice of a house. That's right, it was just a block away from the cemetery. or perhaps two blocks. It's not such a bad thing after all that the bus is going so slowly; it's like going on a tour of the district again, street by street.

Just think, I know this area like the back of my hand. Twenty years ago all this was countryside, you'd never believe it now. As kids we used to play on the open ground behind the butcher's. The boys would make two goalposts out of old planks to play football, and would let us girls join in only if we begged and hassled them. Any girl fortunate enough to be allowed to play would be given the job of fetching the ball every time it went over the line. The poor thing would have to run here, there and everywhere, tongue lolling, except for the rare occasions when the ball landed in the butcher's backyard. In which case it was a job for one of the boys, who had to brave the butcher's wrath as he stood arms akimbo over his greasy circular saw, and keep out of the way of the dog tied up at the end of the yard, baying mournfully at the smell of the hanging carcasses. But apart from the butcher's yard and the dog's unrelieved desolation, the street was quiet and respectable. There can't have been more than four or five one-storey houses, with their little gardens sheltered by the mahogany trees that later were cut down. The few times I've seen the house since, unlike the other houses which have fallen into disrepair, it looked smarter and prettier than when we lived there, probably because the owner who claimed it back for her own use planted some jasmine over the porch. But the extraordinary thing is I can barely reconstruct the rooms inside the house, despite having lived there for over fifteen years. It must be because my mother never opened the shutters; as far as she was concerned the sun was enemy number one, the light faded the chintz chaircovers, and dust had to be avoided like the plague. Ocassionally I would slip into the dark sitting room and flop on to the settee. I can remember the urgency with which I would search, in vain, for some hint of warmth or softness. The settee was as cold and hard as stone, and in the murky light my fingers would rub against the rough edges of the little crochet mats protecting the arms. I would always run out of the sitting room before my eyes had had time to get used to the dark; so I never found out quite what that inner sanctum so jealously guarded by my mother looked like. When I think about it, I'm amazed at the thought that my father and I should have submitted to that absurd tyranny; perhaps we felt anything was better than the interminable recriminations my mother would heap upon us. To get from the front door to the kitchen, the bedrooms or the bathroom, we would have to skate along on the pieces of felt always waiting for us by the front door, like cats. If when you came in the felt skates were in use, you would wait patiently till the other person had finished with them and sent them skidding down the hall along the polished floor. My father and I would go along with all sorts of ridiculous fads like that, just to keep her quiet. The odd thing is, it didn't bring the two of us together. I sensed at an early age that my father would rather have had a boy than a girl, and that he felt his life was totally ruined by having to share it with two useless females. When I think now of the things the two of us had to put up with, I can see why the derelict playground outside was paradise to me, and why my father became another person when he crossed the threshhold of the café. We put up with the polenta and minestrone in the blistering heat of summer, the permanent darkness, the orders not to go into certain taboo areas of the house, including the carved mahogany dining room that was never used, just as the drinks cabinet, whose glint would suddenly catch my eye in the gloom, was never opened. Life was in the street; people talking and even replying to you, light, sun, noise. Why I want to see it again, I can't imagine. We've gone past it and I missed it; the lights must be out. All the lights are out nowadays in Montevideo, even the streetlights. The cemetery must be like the jaws of hell. I should have told Irene the story of how I first met Luisa; it would have amused her. I realise now I hardly opened my mouth the whole afternoon, though it must be said she didn't give me much of a chance. She can't have talked to anyone for ages. Let me think, Irene: Luisa must have been about thirty or thirty-five when we met. I swear. I was just a little girl, you see, and something made me go up to the group of people she was with because it was unusual to see people going for a stroll in the cemetery as if down the main street. What was I doing in the cemetery? Haven't you ever been there? In summer the cemetery was a fabulous garden, better than any park; at the end of the avenue of cypress trees you could see the river curving away into the distance, and on either side it was surrounded by wonderful, enormous trees smothered in red and green ivy. You couldn't even see the graves for the thick tangle of morning-glory. You must remember the morning-glory! The only places I've been to are Montevideo and Buenos Aires, but I think I can safely say there are few things in the world as beautiful as a carpet of morning-glory. No, I didn't play with other children in the cemetery; they were scared of the graves, morning-glory or no morning-glory. I used to go in the late afternoon, when it started to get cool, and that way I also avoided clashing with the funeral that took place at midday. In the late afternoon the keepers were busy drinking maté and kept out of the way. Now I'll tell you how I first set eyes on Luisa. She was the only woman in a group of about six or seven people, that was the first thing that attracted my attention. Later I looked at them more carefully and discovered another one, wearing trousers and a dark blue blouse, who I hadn't noticed at first. But no one could have failed to notice Luisa. I'd never seen anyone dressed like that before, being used to the flowery housecoats my mother and the neighbours wore all the time, you can imagine. Luisa was wearing a printed chiffon dress full of flounces that rippled as she walked, and a floppy, wide-brimmed hat which, whenever there was a gust of wind, she would steady with a stylish flourish of her arm. Nor had I ever seen an arm so white. You must be thinking I can't possibly remember all those details. Who knows, maybe I've embroidered the scene over the years. But I don't think so; what I do remember quite clearly is the incredible impression Luisa made on me, an apparition flitting through the graveyard. Every now and then she would lean on a tombstone as, with her foot, she opened up a path through the trails of morning-glory. In the wind, I could only hear snatches of what she was saying. I hadn't the faintest idea what she was up to, and I suppose it was only when I grew up that I realised she'd been reciting something. It was totally ridiculous, I quite agree. Perhaps if it happened now I'd die of laughing. But maybe not, remember the night you met her… For me, at the time, she was simply fascinating, and so it seemed she was to her companions, who were following behind like retainers. It's possible that Luisa had such panache she could get away with doing the most bizarre things without it entering anyone's head to smile. Even from a distance her voice was loud and clear; I could distinguish the individual words perfectly. Was that the moment I discovered words could have a life of their own, and could exist on a different plane from my mother's endless strings of complaints or my schoolteacher's steely, mechanical exhortations? I don't know. Maybe I'm idealising Luisa too, who's to say. But let's get back to the story. All of a sudden, something magical happened: a gust of wind snatched the hat off her head but she, raising her white arm imperiously, stopped her companions from running after it. With the other hand she slowly let down her hair, loosely knotted at the back of her neck. Her hair started to billow out behind her as the hat blew over the carpet of morning-glory. Without thinking, I started to run as fast as my legs would carry me till, threading my way through the tombstones, I managed to grab hold of it just as it was about to blow off again. I couldn't believe how soft it was in my hand; nothing like the bobbles on my mother's crochet mats. I put it on and made my way

115

towards the group of people; it was the first act of daring I'd committed in my life, you know how shy I am. The hat came down over my ears and I must have been a pretty comic sight because the men started to laugh, and the goddess stepped down from the tomb on which she'd been standing and her voice, so close to me, sent tremors down my spine. I couldn't understand a word of what she was saying, it was probably something quite ordinary. I had the impression she was telling me to keep the hat, but I insisted on giving it back to her, till she took it back and tied it to her belt by the ribbon. I can't tell you how long I went on savouring my moment of glory, poring over every detail. Each time I'd imagine her saying something different to me and the words would have the effect of a spell. Luisa went on talking to me, but I still couldn't understand a word. I plucked up courage to come out with the one set phrase I'd been taught and said: 'My name's Dolores'. I don't know why that should have produced mirth all round but she, with an entirely straight face, unlike the others, gave me her hand and we walked together down the avenue to the main gate. Then I ran off. But that's not the end of the story. Believe it or not, the episode stayed in Luisa's mind too. Almost ten years later I saw her again in the Athenaeum. As always, she was holding court amid a group of admirers. She suddenly saw me and made her way over to me saying: 'You're the girl in the cemetery, aren't you? What was your name?' I was struck dumb and barely managed to stammer a reply: 'Dolores!' She exclaimed, 'That's right, Dolores!' Like you, she had the ability to make the person she was speaking to feel he or she was unforgettable; don't get cross now, maybe it's actually true, it's just that it's hard to believe when you feel so dull and ordinary. The net result was that I submitted to her yoke, like the lion in the national anthem; and she was able to add my name to her long list of vassals. Though she often told me how well she got on with me. And I wasn't to imagine that she got on well with everyone, anything but. She found most people stupid and boring. Sometimes she'd whisper something to that effect in my ear, in the middle of a gathering for whose benefit she was displaying her usual range of seductive charms. I didn't take her too seriously, knowing how she was always trying to get attention by coming out with some unexpected line. Some people are like that, always one step ahead. I'm just the opposite, as you know.

When things started to get bad, Luisa's camp-followers became a more mixed and even ragged bunch. Who wants to talk about poetry when you can be stopped on any streetcorner by an army patrol asking to see your papers, with the power to do whatever they want with you? But it was amazing how rapidly Luisa adjusted to the realisation that imagination, the ability to create new worlds, had passed into another camp; that's to say, it had been appropriated by young people for practical purposes. For no less a purpose than that of inventing a better country than the one they were living in. So while other people of her age took refuge in nostalgia for the Montevideo of the past, she switched tack overnight and drew up a new cast of supporting actors, surrounding herself with young people. The consequences for me were amusing because, having previously been regarded as the regimental mascot, I now became the marshal of the new recruits. Luisa's seductive tactics also changed; she set herself up in the role of guardian angel and co-conspirator, thereby winning over even the sceptics and fanatics. In her new incarnation, she spared only a few old admirers, or rather exlovers, among them Herrera, the Commissioner of Police, though in his case she kept telling us jokingly it was worth her while to keep him in bed so we'd have a good alibi. Poor Luisa, she over-estimated her power over him! When it came to the fateful party you attended, the Commissioner of Police showed his true colours; he behaved like a shit of the first order who didn't care a damn about the romance of the imagination, as Luisa used to call it.

Wait a bit, we're going past the cemetery. You can't see a thing, not even the railings. A little while ago they boarded them up from the inside with corrugated iron. That's all the brutes are good for, walling things up. God knows what they're trying to keep out, at this stage in the proceedings. Even they're not fully satisfied that they've succeeded in wiping out the revolution, those who support the revolution, those who sympathise with the revolution, and finally those who by their silence fail to oppose the revolution, to quote a well-known criminal at the helm of a certain neighbouring nation.

I should have told Irene all that, instead of keeping it to myself. I'm still useless when it comes to talking, I never seem to get beyond monosyllables. Andrés and Victoria used to say the less you talked, the better. A generation of dumb idiots. Irene and Luisa; I never even had the courage to tell Victoria how I'd fallen under her spell. How could I explain to her that Luisa, strolling through the cemetery, or Irene, in the empty theatre in Montevideo rehearsing the cabaret that was never put on, are my fantasy world, my nocturnal apparitions, the unexpressed passion that runs through the lines of my poems, the irremediable suspicion that my slice of the cake is the worst of all possible worlds.

I can't quite remember whether it was Luisa who got me out of prison that time. I think it must have been, because she was waiting for me in the room outside, with the corporal whose job it was to return my documents and bag to me. On the way out, she kept asking me what they'd done to me. Because she'd kick up a hell of a stink if…! She too still believed there were such things as laws in Uruguay. And we still believed it when we went with Luisa's lawyers to try to secure the release of the others who were still in jail. The two of us even went to see Herrera, with whom she'd broken after that ill-starred night. He greeted us with his usual charm. We had to realise that there was a serious problem of overcrowding in the prisons. It was quite conceivable that they might have lost track of the odd prisoner, temporarily at least. Most unfortunate but a fact; he looked sincerely concerned. When we got outside we realised we'd been indulging in amiable party chit-chat, while the others were probably dead. Luisa burst into tears. Black mascara stains were dribbling down her cheeks. She got out a hankie and powder-compact and assiduously mopped her face, but she couldn't stop crying. Without make-up her face looked drawn, as if it were a mask. I stared at my feet, so as not to be party to her sudden demise. She put her arm round me, and we carried on walking aimlessly round the streets. All our efforts were in vain. By that time I didn't even know where Enrique was. Almost two years later, Herrera sent Luisa a card; it was the official notification authorising her to reclaim the body and bury it, with his kind regards. That same night Enrique's photo was one of those shown on television. The next morning, first thing, she rang me, came round and showed me the card. She knew me well enough to know I wouldn't create a scene or get hysterical. I'd known for a long time that it was a fight to the death, but the card still weighed like lead in my hand. I couldn't get over the fact that the message was written by hand and that it was Luisa who'd been authorised to bury Enrique. Did that mean that, after all that had happened to me, they regarded me as clinically dead, to use the medical term? Perhaps I was clinically dead... It's odd, but that idea affected me more than Enrique's death. A corporal had to accompany us and no other mourners were permitted; a few days later, the corporal appeared at the door. She'd greased his palm, as you can imagine, and he'd agreed to keep quiet if I came too. She stood at my side and took my head in her hands and leant it gently against her perfumed dress, and I put my arms round her waist and held her tight and we stood there sealed in an embrace that was tighter even than the seal on the coffin, till the corporal coughed and muttered that he couldn't hang around waiting any longer. We got into the army truck together with the coffin. It was tiny, made of unvarnished wood. Enrique wasn't very tall, more or less my size; but he couldn't possibly have fitted in that coffin; the idea obsessed and tormented me. The truck drove

119

through the gates and up the central driveway of the new cemetery; a horrible, bare open space, with not so much as a shrub in sight. The grave had been dug ready waiting for us; two soldiers clumsily lowered the coffin into it, under the corporal's supervision. Before we'd had time to register what was happening, the hole had been filled in and levelled down. The corporal asked us if we wanted a lift home, and as we didn't answer turned his back on us and marched off. Luisa went to find a stone among the weeds growing over the other graves and pressed it into the newly dug earth, as if to mark the spot. It seemed a pointless gesture. I don't believe in visiting the dead. I felt numb, completely numb. We left, her hand resting gently on my shoulder. I suddenly remembered the afternoon I'd first met her and she'd walked down the cypress avenue with me to the gates of the old cemetery. But the driveway where we were walking now was chalky white, flanked by grotesque memorials. I felt ashamed of my lack of emotion and tried to provoke a reaction of grief. I kept on saying silently to myself that I'd just buried my husband, that gentle, soft-spoken man who'd respected and protected me, who'd been worried by the thought of bringing a child into the world in times like these, but who'd been wild with delight when he found out. And yet no reaction; I kept going over the whole story again and again, as if it were someone else's story, anyone's story. Then suddenly, for no apparent reason, I doubled up and fell on my knees on that ghoulish white driveway, howling like an animal. I howled and howled, and Luisa held me and went on holding me without saying a word or trying to stop me, though not a single soul came out to see what was happening in that plaster-white desert.

The minute Dolores got to Buenos Aires, they told her not to stop even to unpack her things; they'd be leaving that same afternoon. She was pleased they'd waited for her to get there so she could accompany Victoria. There wasn't much of a risk involved; it was quite plausible that a nearly qualified biologist should travel to a settlement in Patagonia, and even more plausible that she should take a friend with her. Besides, you could bank on the constant cock-ups made by the police, military and paramilitary spy networks, not to mention individual informers, neighbours, etc.; the anti-terrorist squads had multiplied to such an extent and reached such a state of sophistication that they were teetering on the brink of chaos. All this was going through Dolores's mind as she surveyed the room where they'd arranged for her to stay. She lay back on the bed by the phone, next to her closed suitcase. She looked at her watch; still more than an hour to go before Victoria was due to come and fetch her. Would they go by train? She was filled with a sense of release unlike anything she'd felt for a long time, as if about to go on holiday, and shut her eyes trying to hold on to the feeling. She was fed up with her life being ruled, since she came out of hospital, by the fear that was always lurking just beneath the surface. She didn't believe those people who claimed they'd got over their sense of fear, and that torture wasn't that bad really. How could anyone who'd experienced it talk like that? She was permanently obsessed by fear of being arrested again; anything was preferable to that. And by anything she meant death. Why wasn't she brave enough to carry a poison capsule around with her, as so many others did, in case she found herself unavoidably cornered? She'd have to pluck up courage to do it. The one thing she was sure of was that she couldn't take being in prison again, going back into a room like the previous one, hearing the order to get undressed, feeling the pain of the first kick in the ribs. Or maybe this time they'd give her electric shocks... How many times had she told herself angrily she must stop thinking about it? Was there no way of escaping the hell that was memory? She buried her head under the pillow and started to count up to a hundred, gritting her teeth. On other occasions she would mutter a prayer that came to her out of the blue, or simply hurl curses and insults into the empty air. The exertion would make the fear recede into the distance, but as soon as she stopped to catch her breath, drained by the effort, it came silently creeping back.

Victoria arrived exactly on time.

'I've brought some sweaters for you because we'll freeze to death down there, but I can see they won't fit in your case. Let's put them in my bag.'

'Is it cold at this time of year?'

'It's always cold there. Well, that's what I've been told, I've never been before. Two of the students in my year are down at the settlement. One of them can be trusted, it's best to steer clear of the other one. But there's plenty of time for me to put you in the picture, we've got an eight-hour train journey ahead of us. It's not exactly going to be a holiday, don't get the wrong idea; I'm afraid we've got to be back by Friday.'

As they went downstairs, Dolores worked out that today was Tuesday so…'Only two days, oh no, don't tell me…' She felt as disappointed as when her parents announced to her as a schoolgirl that it was the end of the holidays. It was idiotic to be thinking in terms of a holiday. Was Victoria likely to do anything for the sole reason of pleasing her? Was she likely to do anything just for pleasure? Forget it! Though there would be more than enough time to find out on the journey, supposing she did feel like opening up. The truth was that since she'd taken over from Andrés as leader of the group, she'd behaved with clockwork precision, caution and efficiency. 'Quite right too,' Dolores thought. 'Otherwise the group would have fallen apart at the seams.' When Victoria replaced Andrés and the other two dead comrades, everyone observed that she knew exactly what she was doing and that she was acting as Andrés' stand-in. The same clipped, contained vehemence, and the same intelligence in translating it into action. And to complete the similarity, shortly after the disaster the old doctor had reappeared at her side; although it was clear his son's death had dealt him a mortal blow, the projection of his son's personality on to

Victoria allowed him to endure his remaining years with dignity.

On the journey, as she'd hoped, they talked at length, as never before. Victoria became more expansive. Inevitably, the subject of families came up and, to Dolores's surprise, she showed a genuine respect for her father.

'Of the two of them,' she explained to her, 'I know of course that Elena is the one I can trust, because she's flexible enough to modify her way of looking at things; with a bit of mental effort, she can accept the concept of radical social change. Whereas for my father it's out of the question; that's why I feel so sorry for him. If what he calls the established order were to cease to function, it would be the end of the world for him, total collapse. And he'd do everything in his power to see that the rules of the game were re-established. For example, I was meant to go to the States to do my doctorate like my brother, and marry a lawyer or a distinguished doctor, because he'd patiently prepared the ground, leaving no stone unturned, so things would turn out that way.'

'Which is more or less the way you work in the group.'

Victoria looked at her and fell silent for a moment.

'Not more or less. Exactly the same. I work in just the same way as he does. That sounds awful, doesn't it? And he can't accept the fact that, when the two of us have exactly the same working methods and routine, we can come to such diametrically opposed results. He feels like someone who's spent the whole of his life constructing the perfect building, and along comes his daughter and blows it all up with a bomb that is just as perfect and just as well-constructed. Do you see what I mean?'

'I'm not too happy with your example. You make it sound as though he was right and you were some kind of lunatic.'

'If I put it like that it's because I'm talking to you,' Victoria protested. 'I don't have to explain to you how the prosperity of the ruling classes is founded on exploitation and poverty, do I? Don't let's get on to that.'

'Going back to my father,' she carried on after a brief pause, 'it never ceases to amaze me that someone so intelligent and brilliant should fail to understand that you can go down the same street in two directions, especially considering the fact that a lot of his colleagues took the opposing path. Did you know that my father and Andrés' father worked together on a couple of legal cases? And look at that wonderful old man...'

'One thing worries me,' Dolores interrupted. 'Your father can only see the arrow pointing right, okay. But what about the people who only see the arrow pointing left?'
'That's not so bad,' Victoria replied with a smile. 'But it's a mistake too; what I mean is that your position is strategically unsound, because you over-estimate your strength and fail to appreciate that of the enemy. Which happens with us quite a lot, as you know. Andrés always used to say that you have to beware of two dangers: sentimentalism and improvisation. If you add dogmatism to the list, you've more or less isolated the three main problems.'

'But if you keep emotion, spontaneity and passionate conviction under check, what are you left with? Aren't you going to end up with a pretty inhuman specimen?'

'You're left with Andrés,' Victoria said. 'Have you ever known anyone more human than Andrés?'

I was in Montevideo at the time Andrés was killed. I found out over the phone, as usual, when someone rang advising me to postpone my trip to Buenos Aires, subject to further notice. So it was almost a month before I was able to go back, and I found Victoria installed as leader of the group. There were three other new members, two boys and a girl. I took to the girl. She was a shop steward in the textile workers' union, serious and quiet. The boys were too young for my liking. I felt things were starting to go the way they'd gone in Montevideo, with new recruits who were less and less experienced and, worse still, more and more inclined to act

124

off their own bat as the heads of their elders started to roll. But the other comrades reassured me and I realised they had total faith in Victoria's judgement. I discovered it had been Andrés who, anticipating his death as he anticipated everything, had decreed that Victoria should take over the leadership from him. They told me that Andrés had been against the assault, but the orders had come from above and had to be carried out. Initially he had entrusted the operation to three other members of the group, but then, quite unexpectedly, decided to take part himself; now they realised he knew it was going to be a failure and didn't want to send three people to their deaths. Though who was to say what the real reason had been? The operation went wrong just as he'd maintained it would, but there was no point in recriminations now. No one ever found out exactly how they died either. The military reports are always worded in the same way: 'The following terrorists were killed while attempting a raid...'

'When none of them got back,' Victoria said, 'I took a taxi and went straight to Andrés' parents' house. They were in the middle of dinner, and one of his brothers came to the door. As soon as I appeared in the doorway, his father got up and slammed his hands down on the table. How long had he been waiting in agony for something of the kind? I stammered a few words, I can't even remember what. I think I said I suspected something had gone wrong. His mother let out a scream and the children gathered round her. I went up to his father and said that, regardless of what had happened, we had to wait and see. We waited up all night. In the early hours of the morning, another member of the group sent a message to say that the three of them had been killed. I don't know whether it was because we'd been hardened by the interminable expectation of death, but I have to confess the confirmation of the news was less terrible than I'd expected. Andrés' father and I were alone in the dining room.

We stayed there, without stirring. Every now and then one of the children would come in with some coffee and we would exchange a few words. None of the three children could stop crying, it was incredible; they kept tiptoeing in and out of the bedroom where they'd forced his mother to go and lie down, after making her take some tranquilisers. At seven there was a phone call from the police, asking a member of the family to come to identify the body. I thanked God we'd always insisted on everyone carrying on their person full details of their next of kin, in case anyone stopped to take pity on them lying wounded or dead. At least that way we knew what was what.'

She fell silent, looking out of the window at the passing landscape, and said no to the cigarette Dolores offered.

'I went with Andrés' father most of the way to the morgue, but then we had to separate as a safety measure. I could feel the tears running down my cheeks as I watched the old man from behind, walking slowly and deliberately, hugging the walls of the houses. And at the same time I felt relieved not to have to see Andrés lying under a sheet, riddled with bullets.'

'It's worse imagining things,' Dolores said after a bit.

Victoria looked at her and she felt the intense warmth of her gaze and thought that people do not die in vain. She thought there was still room for love in this world, and felt so humble and grateful she could have fallen on her knees at Victoria's feet.

'Yes,' she replied, 'it's worse imagining things.'

They stayed silent for some time. Victoria was going through a notebook methodically, making an occasional note in the margin. Dolores tried to read, but found it difficult to concentrate. Before she'd been a voracious reader, but she hardly ever read a book nowadays. She could never manage to get through more than a few lines at a time without other thoughts crowding into her head and taking over. She would feel like telling them to go away, but would not have the energy either to expel them or to clarify them. The images

126

clamouring for attention would leave her exhausted. Would there ever be an end to this, once it was all over? The situation in Montevideo was totally unfavourable to continuing the armed struggle. The domino theory was proving itself correct and whole groups at a time were falling like ninepins. In Buenos Aires, however, there was less of an imbalance of forces. On the contrary the movement was growing, though the chaos was growing at a similar rate. On both sides people had taken to acting of their own accord and at their own peril. Both the dictators and the leaders of the resistance were finding themselves overtaken by those who wanted to take justice into their own hands. Fear of losing made people more impatient, which led to increased losses; a perfect vicious circle. But, in this deadly stalemate, the dice were loaded. The police and the army, the assassins and the torturers had a clear advantage; any paramilitary outrage could be justified in the name of the dirty war. From the moment the enemy invented that phrase, Dolores thought, it had ceased to be a war and had become a bloodbath; there would be no more mercy, no more trials, it was the end of the myth of legality and '*l'imagination au pouvoir*'. To start with, the change was imperceptible. Victoria had still thought she was obeying the rules of combat when she travelled to the south of the country to make contact with the members of the movement there. Had death entered into her calculations? Dolores couldn't fathom it out and studied her face as she went on writing in her notebook, fascinated by her distant yet vehement beauty. She was wearing her hair loose and it cascaded over her shoulders, enveloping her like a cape, giving her the irretrievably archaic look of a figure from a Pre-Raphaelite painting.

The two boys waiting for them at the settlement bundled them into the jeep. They said nothing till they got on to the main road. 'The hut is about twenty minutes' drive from here,' the one at the wheel said. None of them made another move to speak. Dolores was looking out of the window, but there was little point because it was pitch dark. There was no sign of habitation. The jeep started to climb and almost instantly they pulled up in front of the hut. The boy next to the driver leapt to the ground, helped them get out and opened the door of the hut, with Dolores following behind. He deposited the bags on the table and lit an oil lamp hanging from the ceiling. It was bitter cold, but the boy turned on a heater and the warmth started to seep into the room. Then he showed her the tiny kitchen and opened the bathroom door so she could take a look. 'You can put a candle in there,' he said, and started to rummage around in a drawer but changed his mind, opened the pantry door and showed her the pile of tins inside. 'There's no fresh food,' he explained, 'but it'll do for a couple of days, won't it?' Dolores started to get fed up with him showing her round and explaining where everything was as if they'd come to a hotel and she was a wealthy client. What had he taken her for? She started to open her case for the sake of doing something, and the boy took advantage of the gesture to bid her a hasty good-bye and go back to the jeep. Dolores peered out of the window and saw that Victoria had moved into the front seat and was engaged in animated conversation with the boy at the wheel. When the other boy opened the door, he put his arm round her and they went on talking for a bit longer, but as the boy outside was jumping up and down to keep warm, Victoria said goodbye to both of them and came indoors. 'I'm going to be in their way,' Dolores thought, feeling more and more mortified. It hadn't been her idea to come, after all, and now she was going to have to put up with being treated like a cumbersome object. Victoria made sure the door was locked and started to look round the hut, completely oblivious to her companion's feeling. She put the notebooks and coats down on a chair and started to inspect the pantry, open the drawers, feel the matresses, look out of the window screening her eyes with both hands. She chose the top bunk and said that what was needed, right away, was a good, hot coffee. And then a hearty meal. Dolores needn't worry, she was an excellent cook. She started to hum as she laid the cups and sugar bowl out on the table and Dolores stood watching her in amazement. What on earth was going on? Why this sudden elation that seemed so out of character? She went on staring at her, hands in her pockets, rooted to the ground, but as Victoria passed her on her way to open her bag she grasped her firmly by the shoulders and gave her a shake. What was the matter? Didn't she think the hut was wonderful? Wasn't she happy at the thought of two days' holiday, even if it was only two days? 'Well I am, so there,' Victoria declared without waiting for her to reply. 'I can't even remember when I last had a holiday. And there's no one for miles around, just think. No one outside, no one threatening you, no one spying on you. No one to give you orders, no one to make you do anything. And tommorow we'll drag you off for a walk, like it or not, and to hell with the cold. We're near the beach, apparently the sea's within walking distance.' Dolores finally succumbed to her euphoria; the feeling of constriction across her chest began to ease and she allowed herself to let go. When would she be meeting the other members of the group, she asked Victoria. 'Tomorrow and the day after, in the evening. That's the only possible time of day,' she replied. 'The meetings will take place here.' Dolores detected a certain flatness creeping into Victoria's voice, but she immediately brightened up and jauntily said why didn't they forget about all that, they weren't to talk about anything serious, anything serious was out, they were on holiday. She put her bag on the table and started taking her things out. Dolores leant her elbows on the table, feeling happy. Victoria put two sweaters and a heap of woolly tights in a drawer; then got out a pair of boots, some woolly hats and scarves. See how she'd thought of Dolores, she'd brought two of everything so they could wrap up like Eskimos when they went outside. Dolores peered into the almost empty bag and saw a couple of flannel nightdresses and a teddy bear. The teddy had an ear missing and was threadbare in parts. When Victoria came back over to the table and saw what she was looking at, she went red and burst out laughing, as she tucked the teddy under the nightdresses. 'So you've found out about Ben,' she giggled. 'You won't tell anyone, will you? Promise you won't tell anyone!' Dolores was left speechless again, flabbergasted not so much by Ben and the insistence on her not telling anyone as by Victoria's giggles. She'd never heard her laugh before; she was used to her silent smile but now she was chuckling and giggling uncontrollably like a little girl hiding from her parents behind a chair. Victoria stopped laughing and looked at her. She stretched out her hand and pushed Dolores's black hair back. For the second time Dolores was surprised by the firmness of her touch. 'Well,' Victoria said looking her in the eye, 'what are you so surprised about? We have to act our age sometimes.' She kept her hand on her forehead and studied her face intently, as if looking at her for the first time. 'I'm twenty-two,' she finally said. 'How old are you?' But Dolores didn't answer. She gently picked up the hand holding her hair back and put it on the table. Then she leant her head on it and stayed like that for a moment trying to imagine what it would be like to start to live again, but when she closed her eyes the questions why? when? how? came flooding back and she violently brushed Victoria's hand aside and started to bang her head against the table. It was no use, it was no use, unhappiness had become second nature to her, there was no way she could break the pattern. Ben the teddy bear was no help at all.

The next morning Dolores was the first one up. She leapt out of bed to go to the window. The hut was surrounded by sand dunes on all sides. She went to the door after wrapping one of the woolly jackets round her and saw the track the jeep had come up the night before winding its way downhill over the bare, bleached dunes. She took a few steps outside, hugging herself in the bitterly cold wind, and suddenly the view opened up before her; the sand dunes sloped gently down to a vast beach with the sea shimmering in the distance. An unbroken line of foam ran across the horizon. She felt devastated by the view; it was as if the natural world was destined to wipe the arrogance of man off the face of the earth. But this vision of desolation was as awesome as it was irremediable. Anyway they'd have to learn to live with it because the boys had taken the jeep with them. And how had Victoria. . .? At that moment she heard Victoria calling out to her from the door of the hut. She'd pulled a sweater on over her nightdress and was running in the same posture as herself, protecting herself from the wind. From where she was, Dolores pointed towards the beach. Victoria ran up to her, nodding approvingly, ecstatic with delight. The two of them looked at each other as they stood there hugging themselves, teeth chattering, and burst out laughing simultaneously. 'Let's get cracking,' Victoria said. 'It'll be boiling later on when the sun gets high in the sky, you'll see.' They set off suitably equipped, after a wholesome breakfast prepared by Victoria. She went on finding everything wonderful and the walk was the adventure she'd been looking forward to for ages. She let her embarrassment about Ben go to the winds and used him as a cushion or as a ball. In fact, after a while running around on the beach they warmed up, and the aimless ramble and Victoria's gaiety infused Dolores with an unexpected vitality. Perhaps it might be possible after all? They discovered there was a lighthouse some way further along the coast, but decided to postpone visiting it till the following day. They got back to the hut exhausted, slightly dazed by the whistling of the wind, and rushed to the kitchen to heat up the coffee. Night fell in a matter of minutes and they'd just finished having a bite to eat when the other members of the group arrived. At the drop of a hat, Victoria switched back to being her usual reserved, inscrutable self, but Dolores no longer cared about being left out of the discussions; besides, she was used to discipline and, in order to avoid any possible embarrasment, climbed into the top bunk and rigged up a candle so she could read. Victoria and the other five sat round the table. They were talking in hushed tones and she couldn't hear what they were saying. The drone of their voices started to lull her to sleep. Every now and then an unexpected noise, someone scraping their chair against the ground or going to the kitchen to stir a saucepan, would wake her up and she would pay attention to what was going on. She could see Victoria reading out to them the instructions jotted in her notebooks, and noting down other instructions in turn. A girl was sitting with her back to her. The light of the oil lamp fell directly on the two boys sitting facing her, elongating their features. One had a red beard, like an Irish sailor; the other was dark and thin, with a delicate profile and a thick moustache. He was smoking non-stop. She didn't want to look at them, because they reminded her of her now defunct group, and on top of that the features of the boy with the moustache were very like those of Enrique. The idea that soon they would all be dead cut through her like a knife. She could barely breathe. She couldn't bring herself to believe that they were sentenced to death for wanting to liberate those who suffered injustice, exploitation and cruelty at the hands of an inhuman system. Was this the monstrous crime they had to pay for with their lives? Why did they have to live in the shadow of death so that others could live to the full and not as hopeless survivors without a future? She, as a hopeless survivor without a future, wanted nothing more than for them to be victorious; but why was it that others felt differently? How could people who were incapable of killing a fly look on impassively, if not smugly, while they were tortured or maimed?

The thoughts started to crowd in on her and, to combat them, shivering, she started to count up to a hundred under her breath.

'I can hardly start screaming and yelling here right now, just think what would happen. Why didn't my mother teach me to pray? I've never known anyone who knew how to pray.'

She was staggered to find herself having such thoughts but didn't want to fall into this new trap and went on counting till she fell into a deep sleep. She was tired — when had she last run around on a beach? When had she last. . .?

The following morning it was she who made the breakfast, shook Victoria who was fast asleep clutching Ben, and chivvied her to get ready so they could walk to the lighthouse. Victoria let her take the initiative and, although she hadn't lost any of her enthusiasm, she looked worried by the previous night's conversation. 'Damn it,' Dolores thought, 'why do we have to live with this bloody mess every day of our lives?' But luckily her companion revived when they got out into the open air and in a matter of minutes her euphoria had returned. They walked along a beach composed not of sand but of millions of shells. They started to fling hundreds of shells at each other, ducking adroitly to get out of the way. Victoria would sometimes sit on the ground and pick one up clumsily with her woolly glove, study it and put it in her pocket. Then she would get up and run over to Dolores. She put her hand on her shoulder.

'Would you like me to give you a zoology lesson?'

'No thanks!' Dolores retorted. 'I bet you don't know the first thing about those creatures and you'll make it all up. If you bore me with zoology, I'll start reciting poetry.'

'I'm an expert at both,' Victoria declared roundly. And started to declaim a string of incomprehensible phrases and facts, but the other girl clamped her hand over her mouth and stopped her from going on.

'All right,' Victoria said, giving in. 'You can stay ignorant if that's the way you want it. How can you write holed up in a room?'

'I don't write about the sea; I'd be running a nine-to-one risk of coming out with the most awful platitudes.'

'Don't you ever write the word sea?'

'Yes, the same as I write the word hell, or fly, or your arm, or whatever. Like any other word, you give it the sense you want it to have.'

'Now then!' Victoria cried, leaping on top of her and putting her hand over her mouth. 'You wouldn't take a lesson from me, I'm not having you give me one.'

She ran up a dune and disappeared down the other side.

A second later her two feet appeared sticking up in the air above the bone-white sand. Dolores laughed out loud and grabbed a handful of shells to bombard her with, but had second thoughts and clambered up the dune after her. Victoria was standing on her head, her arms folded across her chest. 'Yoga,' she said, poker-faced. 'Don't forget I'm from a good family.'

'Now I understand why rich people see everything upside down.'

'Wrong again. This position helps them concentrate on working out what their next move will be. That's why they hardly ever make a mistake. They've got the time and the training.'

'You shouldn't say they never make a mistake, that's asking for trouble.'

'But what if someone of the same ilk were to call their bluff, then what?'

They had to walk some way to get to the lighthouse. Round and stubby, it was perched on a rock overlooking the beach. A narrow stairway leading up to it had been carved out of the rock. From that point the view was daunting. The murky blue sea reflected a cloudless sky. After vainly pushing at the wooden door, they sat down with their backs against the lighthouse wall. Its low windows, boarded up with rusty nails, emphasised the feeling of dereliction. As they looked around them they glimpsed another stairway, slightly wider than the last one, leading down in the other direction to a house that was also clearly abandoned. They got up and started to make their way down. On this side of the rock, they were sheltered from the wind. All that was left of the house were the bare walls, broken floorboards and the lower level of a wooden staircase that somehow had resisted the elements but which, when it got to the first floor, was left hanging in mid-air. Victoria leant against the banisters looking up at a patch of dazzling, clear blue sky, framed by the outline of the walls.

'We're all going to be like this in a little while; skeletons blanched in the wind.'

She said the words in the same jaunty tone of voice she'd kept up throughout the walk. I couldn't take her way of talking and rounded on her viciously, shrieking 'What did you say?'

'Don't get cross with me,' she turned round slowly and looked at me. 'We're not in a committee meeting, are we? Sooner or later they're going to kill us all. You know what death is from your own experience, don't you?'

Why was she still speaking in that cool tone of voice? Why was she stirring up old wounds? 'Unlike you,' I snapped back. I regretted the words as soon as they'd come out but it was too late, and anyway wasn't it true? I realised that deep down I was clinging on to a macabre sort of pride in the two deaths in my life. Sporting them like a rosette. Victoria sat down on one of the steps carved out of the rock and stared fixedly out to sea. Which told me that in a little while she'd start speaking in a quiet, calm voice.

'Let's say for the sake of argument that you're right and I don't have any personal experience of death. But what I was getting at is that we're the losers. Not our parents or our children. But us, just our luck! Andrés would have been a top professional. And so, no doubt, would I. Juan Pablo, a brilliant mathematician. And so would Toni, though not quite so brilliant. You can't imagine how talented Delia is. Let's hope she has time to get her first exhibition.'

She was going through a list of names I didn't know, presumably the people from the previous night; I felt incredibly hurt that I didn't figure anywhere in her count.

'And what about me?' I finally asked angrily.

'You?' She came back to reality and looked me in the face. 'You? What about you?'

I turned away and started to go down the steps back to the beach, but she ran after me and grabbed me by the arm and forced me to face her.

'But don't you see, you've probably come through it all and are out on the other side! I'm not including you because I'd put your name on the list of the living. You can't be angry with me, because you're the only person I've been so frank

135

with for years. And you've got to understand that I want to go on living, I don't want to die for anything in the world; I'm not sitting here waiting for them to kill me. I'm not bragging about it, I'm afraid. What do you think I'm feeling like inside when I talk about such things?'

The tears were streaming down her face, red with the cold. We hugged each other crying, but we weren't ashamed of it because it could equally well have been because of the cold.

'And if we do come out of this alive,' I could hear Victoria saying in my ear, 'all that's left for us is despair, because in any case we'll be the losers. And that I know is something you've had to face.'

As we made our way down, she went back to thinking aloud.

'You mustn't go around talking like that. Not to anyone, ever. But you have to be aware of it. It's no good believing, like those foolish kids we keep getting landed with, that we're going to win. The only crown we'll win is death. If you know there's a chance you may get killed, you won't feel cheated when it happens. Do you know what the expression is on the face of the boys that keep getting killed every day? One of astonishment. That's something I've talked about a lot with Andrés' father. And he always says that Andrés' face was quite serene. Whereas the young kids think nothing is going to happen to them, like in a TV serial. But this isn't a TV serial.'

I didn't reply. Anything I could have said would inevitably have been coloured by my own experience. At present my life was taken up with trying to forget and trying to get my revenge at the same time, which was an impossibility because, if I was going to get my revenge, then how could I forget? I would make an effort to evoke the image of myself doubled up on the ground, on that chalk-white driveway in the new cemetery, howling my head off for Enrique. Or I would be obliged over and over again to reconstruct the sensation of regaining consciousness in the hospital bed, with my body broken and bruised, attached to a tube pumping liquid into me, gradually coming round in that total whiteness (white wall, white bed, white nurse, white screen round the bed, white bandages, or was it a white straight jacket?), trying ever so slowly to formulate the questions: have-I-had-the-baby? at-what-time-was-it-born? Making ever more desperate efforts to remember, when had I been taken into the hospital? when had the baby been born? where is it? where was I when I was taken to hospital? who took me if it wasn't Enrique? Till, with a sudden, never-abating precision, the image of that room in the prison comes back to me. I lose consciousness. How many times did I lose consciousness in the hospital ward? Days later the nurse told me I seemed to keep coming round and then would fall back into a coma; but what about the baby? Oh that, yes, it was a little girl. Poor little thing, almost completely formed. The nurse was clutching my hand. I realised every time I'd tried to work out why I was there, in that white room, as soon as I got to the scene of the torture chamber my defences would make me fall back into unconsciousness. Till my body regained its strength and was forced to come out of the other end of the tunnel. The nurse is kind and impressionable; I come out of the tunnel clutching her sympathetic hand. But if any of the hospital staff come in, she drops my hand as if it were a hot brick and gets on with her business, ignoring me completely. But my hand is as cold as ice, nothing will ever succeed in warming it.

The bus limped into the bus station en route and the driver got up, stretched and got out to report on the journey. I looked behind me and counted a total of six people. I hadn't even noticed them get on.

How incredible that it should have taken me till this afternoon to fill in the details of Victoria's arrest in the penthouse. I learnt she'd been arrested when they rang me to tell me to stay in Montevideo till the climate got better. I looked out of the window and saw an immaculate cobalt-blue sky. Till the climate got better? That's right, postpone any plans for travel till you hear from us. I shivered. I heard nothing more and grew more and more anxious till people at this end confirmed that she'd disappeared. Which was worse than being in prison. Simply disappeared. As Irene told me all the details, I could imagine the terrible, overpowering fear that must have seized her. Did her father realise he was sentencing her to death by handing over the parcel? Did he want to clear himself of any suspicion of involvement? Who knows. When I think of how Victoria had spoken up in defence of her father, and yet he'd behaved like an out-and-out shit . . . He and his son, two birds of a feather.. Thank God someone in the family behaved decently. But I can't imagine Elena upbraiding her husband and son, or leaving the penthouse, even less moving into that attic in the Calle San Martín. It's amazing! But it has to be said that all three women are pretty amazing when you stop to think about it: Irene walled up in her house by the sea, waiting for news of her son missing in Santiago. Elena, as a result of all this, having got herself involved with the Madwomen of the Plaza de Mayo; and how can I forget all that Luisa did? When you think you'd expect to see them in some elegant tea room chatting to each other about their wonderful finds. (Again she's infuriated by the thought that the three of them would go to any length to track down a colonial angel or a pre-Columbian sculpture.) They were born to be ladies of leisure, to drift through life, to lead an unreal existence. If their bodies were mutilated and thrown into the river, as happens nowadays, you'd recognise them by the jade or quartz pendants hanging round their necks. And wasn't Victoria's lifestyle basically the same? The first time I went to the studio in San Martín, she told me she'd been busy scraping the windowpanes and painting the walls round the platform white. She'd put a Calchaqui rug on the floor, to cover the stains. Next to the mattress, which must have been left behind by the previous occupants, she'd placed a Chinese lacquer coffee table. She showed me round with a slight look of embarrassment on her face and, to pre-empt any criticism on my part, pointed out an angel dressed like a pageboy with a sword in his hand. He was literally holding court on the wall facing the matress. 'I sneaked him out of my parents' house,' she blushed. 'He's from Quito, isn't he beautiful?' He made no impression on me whatsoever. Besides, it irritated me that she wanted to preserve something of the sophisticated atmosphere she was used to. The lower part of the studio was like a pigsty, but the mezzanine was an entirely different world. I squatted on the mattress looking at the angel; how do the wealthy always manage to invent something they can cling to? It took me a long time to come to understand her and learn to condone such concessions on her part. Now it makes me blush to think how inflexible I used to be about stupid things like that.

Seeing Irene again stirred up whole areas of my life that had been blotted out. And when I think now of the passionate response she produced in me the first time we met, I can feel my cheeks burning with the same fire. What sort of passion was it? I never had time to discuss it with Enrique, who was so broad-minded and good at understanding the different kind of relationships one could have with people. He accepted my sudden dislikes, my silences and my unwarranted surliness as signs of an inability to express my feelings; he convinced me they weren't irremediable flaws but that it was just that I haven't been offered any other models of behaviour. He believed in me, poor Enrique. The first and only person to believe in me, perhaps... It's a relief to think of Enrique openly, to think about him as if he were here right now and still the incredible person he was. The best thing he ever did for me, when we first met, was to drag me away from the coldness and emptiness of my parents' house and take me off to the heated atmosphere of the café. He would get up whenever I came in, to make sure everyone greeted me respectfully. Shy, thoughtful and caring, incapable of shouting people down and laughing at them, unlike everyone else. Never putting himself first, as others did. He was always defending someone or something: his teachers, people's parents, institutions, political programmes; the last thing you'd have expected him to turn into was a revolutionary. He steered me towards a new way of life without my even realising. To everyone's surprise, including my own, I became a writer, and people took me seriously. And that gave me a sense of well-being, of self-esteem, in short, a sense of direction. The only problem was his over-protective widowed mother, prepared to put up with anything for the sake of her only son and always on the lookout for trouble. Which is the way to bring it on yourself, of course. Though Enrique was wonderful with her too; he managed to keep her out of our way, what with her bridge parties with her friends and the cake shops; we had a right to our own life and she could grumble as much as she liked but she had to put up with it.

Again she wonders: how many times could it happen? If she loved Enrique, how could she have fallen head-over-heels in love with Irene? Why was it that she couldn't bear to be parted from certain female friends, when she couldn't live without Enrique either? With a disgruntled feeling she reviewed the erratic course of her emotions, which fluctuated in obedience to an unrelieved conviction that she was doomed to unhappiness. How could she make sense of the fact that she felt enslaved by her momentary passions and liberated by her love for Enrique? The image of Irene that night, striding across the stage in the empty theatre, came back to her. So utterly shameless in her long scarlet stockings, as if the world were at her feet. And from that moment everything else ceased to matter; there was no point in living or moving or breathing unless Irene looked at her, noticed her, singled her out.

We agreed to meet next morning at the University. No, it was no trouble at all, she happened to have a class then anyway. Why didn't they have a coffee together? Of course she'd show her where the theatre director's office was.

She was already waiting for me at the entrance to the faculty building by the time I got there; she must have been absolutely frozen standing out there in the cold. The front entrance faces the docks, with a vast open space beyond, fenced off by wire netting, leading to the waterfront. But she was smiling as if impervious to the icy wind, in a lavender, fluffy wool coat so short it looked like a blouse. She couldn't have been more inappropriately dressed, not only because of the weather but also to go round the university, which was no longer the luxury hotel it had been in the past. No sooner had we got to the far end of the entrance hall than we were met by the blast of the gale-force winds pounding round the courtyards, but she strode in unabashed, as if gliding over the antique rugs of the old hotel. I prayed to God that the students wouldn't greet her with wolf whistles, but then realised the courtyards were deserted and they must be at a meeting in the café out on the roof, which had become a kind of permanent debating chamber. Since the unrest had started two months before, there was hardly a lecture that was not disrupted at some point. The lecturers and the administrative staff took to staying away; I thought it highly unlikely we'd find the theatre director in his office, there was never a soul around. But she seemed totally confident that everything would go according to plan and if it didn't, as turned out to be the case, it didn't matter in the slightest. It was wonderful to be with someone so sure of herself, in the midst of the surrounding uncertainty and chaos. She was genuinely delighted by the old hotel; she kept looking around her, pointing out the metal framework overhead, regretting the fact that the courtyards were no longer covered over by glass; she conjured up a palace from out of the ruins and I too started to see it emerge from the peeling walls, the broken glass, the twisted metalwork, the condemned catwalks. In the meantime we were getting frozen as we stood looking down, evoking the palace, her flimsy coat wrapped tightly round her. I took her by the hand and led her to the director's office, but predictably, he wasn't there. She shrugged her shoulders

141

and we went back downstairs. She was looking around her at the marble stairway sprayed with graffiti. As we were going down, we were overtaken by a group rushing out into the street, arguing noisily. One of them grabbed me by the arm and stopped me to ask a question; but all I could think of was the fact that I'd lost sight of her. She must have carried on ahead, but I couldn't find her anywhere in the faculty building or outside in the street. I was incredibly upset that she hadn't waited for me. Hadn't she understood then? Didn't she realise how much I needed her?

It was like a miracle finding her again in the afternoon, standing on her own in the middle of the main street with the same lavender coat and scarlet stockings and elegant high-heeled shoes, just as the military started to close in on us. She was obviously checking to see where the army was advancing from, in order to work out which way to run in order to escape their net. Our group had just come running out of Juan's house, trying to make it to the theatre before it was too late; the main body of the demonstration ahead of us had dispersed, it had been a bigger success than expected and there was no point in taking risks at this late stage in the day. I ran out towards her, frantically grabbed her by the arm and pushed her into our midst; we had to get to the back exit before the cloud of gas cleared. We got inside panting and choking, but there was no slowing her down till we were halfway along the corridor leading to the back of the stage. At that point she stopped and leant against the wall, laughing at our frantic escape, while we were coughing and spluttering as if twice her age. Suddenly she stretched out her hand, brushed my hair back — I can see her now — and gave me a kiss on the cheek. 'What would I have done without you, Dolores! You saved my life.' Her cheek was burning and cold at the same time. 'Like an altar,' I thought, 'like an altar where the faithful come to rest their troubled brows.'

As we came out on to the stage and were able to breathe again, and as she went over to a little heater someone had switched on, I started to ask myself feverishly how could one be so in love with somebody one had only met a few hours before? Why did I feel such a desperate need to be beside her at all hours of the day? Why this breathless expectancy? Even before I'd formulated the questions, I knew they had no answer. It was not the first time I'd felt this kind of burning attraction, eclipsing everything else around me, but it would always burn itself out equally rapidly, as if it could be only a temporary phenomenon. I realised how little I expected of the object of this uncontrollable desire. It was hard to explain. As if my adoration were self-sufficient. Was it the constant, unrelieved drudgery of my life that made me succumb, time and time again, to these sudden, shortlived, obsessions? I knew that Irene was about to go back to Buenos Aires, especially with the chaos in Montevideo, and would then set off on one of her tours, and I would almost certainly never see her again. But it was enough for me to have known her. Irene was always at the centre of things, while I was on the periphery. Exceptional events were the bread and butter of her life. And she still has that power to transform everything into an exceptional event. She proved that today. The few hours I spent with her this afternoon were enough to conjure up all the terrible things that have happened over these past few years, spread before me like a deck of cards. It's incredible! This graveyard suddenly lit up with an unknown light. The disasters in my life no longer looked like lifeless sepulchres but like radiant objects. For a moment she managed to convince me that living in hell is better than living in a no-man's-land. Anything is better than living in a no-man's land.

Did I give her the impression of being sullen and apathetic as I so often do, much to my dismay? Why did I feel too inhibited to tell her how well I'd got on with her son in Chile? I've a feeling I said so once in a letter, though she didn't mention it when we were talking. She probably gets so many letters she throws them straight into the wastepaper basket without even reading them. Though, come to think of it, we didn't speak much about her son at all; she didn't avoid the issue but she didn't raise it explicitly either. But you could see it had her on tenterhooks, despite the fact she seems to believe the protective cloak of optimism she carries around with her will shield her from disaster. It's clear that her optimism is based on a passionate, intense need to believe, unlike the silly candles Enrique's mother used to light at church so her son would get out of prison. I was reminded of Enrique's mother because Irene's son was rather like Enrique in his soft-spokenness and delicate physique. At least, from what little I can remember of that wild, action-packed week in Chile. His reserve always had a certain warmth to it, which he no doubt got from his mother, so that, even if he sat there not saying a word, you knew he was giving you support and encouragement. Just like Irene. But, unlike his mother, he would keep drifting off into a dream world of his own, cutting himself off from the world outside. Was it involuntary or did he cultivate it deliberately? He probably savoured his journeys into outer space which, at the same time, gave him a romantic appeal rare in someone so highly politicised. It was a mystery to me why he should have got so involved in politics; nothing in his tastes, his likes and dislikes seemed to incline him in that direction, and yet he had a very clear line on things, much more so than Irene, whose political involvement was dictated by her whims, and who would always end up justifying her changes of mind in the name of some woolly notion of freedom. He would smile when talking about his mother, but would firmly and gently set aside her shining but vague example in order to come out with his own ideas, with a clarity of exposition that made him stand out among those around him.

It was like carnival time in Santiago. Everybody was there, from the four corners of the globe, and despite all the losses we'd sustained with so many people killed, in prison or missing, nothing could tarnish the optimistic mood of that international gathering. We were so used to the need for clandestinity that we couldn't believe we were out on the streets singing and chanting in our hundreds and thousands.

144

We forgot about torture, death and all the rest of it. We danced in circles, as if we'd rediscovered our childhood. What we found hardest to get used to was the fact that we were the city, we were the government, we were the people. It was worth dying to have that experience. When I think about it now with hindsight, I can't understand how we failed to notice all the people glaring at us, spying on us and waiting to take their revenge. (And they got what they wanted; it has to be said that no one succeeded in taking their revenge quite as spectacularly as they were to do.) Freedom went to our heads; we felt we had the right to be provocative and insolent. Why is it only now I remember that man with three elegantly dressed upper-class ladies, round whom we danced in a ring clapping and chanting slogans? Why does the image of their livid faces, their tight-lipped expression of alarm come back to me now so clearly? Too late. There was no controlling the euphoria of that foreign legion which invaded Chile to partake in the joys and tribulations of its new destiny. But Irene's son was different. We would meet every day at the conference, and he would force us to think twice before we opened our mouths. You felt ashamed if you came out with something stupid in his presence, because even if he only shook his head or smiled awkwardly, there was something in the nervous curve of his mouth that brought people to heel and made them see where they were going wrong. The fact of being the only person who remained silent when everyone else was busy shouting gave him an advantage; as did his insistence on always going ahead to check that all was clear before turning into the next street, now that the city was full of *agents provocateurs* lurking round every corner. Every now and then you would hear isolated shots and the metal shutters of the shops clattering to the ground. You would see people lying in the streets — wounded? dead? — and with no one daring to investigate because the spot was a notorious danger-point. While we were blindly dancing in the streets, celebrating the triumph of the revolution. What was her son's name? I've forgotten. Remembering him now, I'd be very surprised if he'd done anything rash in these terrible last few days, especially bearing in mind that he's got a pregnant wife to protect. It's a matter of luck, and in a catastrophe of such magnitude that's something completely outside human control. To think of all those people shot, arrested, tortured, in hiding. . . The silly thing is I can only think of them singing and dancing, even with Santiago in flames around them or patrolled by tanks; another circle of hell we failed to foresee like all the others.

'No one knows what's happened to anyone,' Irene said. 'It's almost better that there should be a total news blackout, for a while anyway; it gives you the impression it's the telephone and telegraph networks that have been destroyed and not the people.'

'Can't you get through by phone?'

'Everything's cut off. Phones, cables, the telexes in the news agencies. The only news is what's broadcast on the radio. And what the radio hams manage to pick up. Yesterday there was a report on the radio of two students waving white handkerchiefs being mown down by machine guns. One of them was a Bolivian boy. It was in the provinces, up in the north.'

'Do you think the coup caught him in Santiago?'

'That's what I'm hoping. If only I had some way of knowing! What I'm afraid of is that they may have gone back to Concepción before the coup, because in the provinces there'll be no mercy. But that's a stupid thing to say; there'll be no mercy in Santiago either; there's been wholesale slaughter in the industrial belts apparently.'

'All I heard about was the Stadium, which they're filling with detainees. If they get arrested, let's hope they get taken there; at least, it'll be safer than being on the streets. Anyway, what can they do with all the hundreds and thousands of people they've rounded up in the Stadium? They'll have to let them out in the end.'

146

'I can't imagine what's happening to them, wherever they are,' Irene said after a pause. 'I simply can't bear to think about it. I'd rather cling to the image of them waving good-bye to me at the airport.'

'When did you leave Santiago?'

'Two days before.'

'What good timing!'

'Bad timing, because I'd rather be there now than be here desperately waiting for news. I'd only be in the way, but at least I'd be with them. I can see them waving till the plane left the runway, clinging to the wire fence. He helped her insert her feet into the holes and held her up as she pressed her already visibly swollen belly against the wire netting, waving goodbye with both hands. I can't explain why the sight of the two of them there affected me so much; it must have been because of her almost apprehensive smile and the lean, hungry look on my son's face, as a result of eating and sleeping less and less well.'

'If all the young people there fit that description, no wonder the coup succeeded.'

Irene smiled.

'I don't know what to say to that, perhaps I'm exaggerating. It was so hard to know what was going on in those last few days; people were rabidly confident and rabidly cynical at the same time.'

'That's not the impression I got when I was in Santiago.'

'When were you there?'

'About a year and a half ago.'

'Of course, I remember the enthusiastic letter you wrote me. It seems funny to think of that now, things were so different then.'

'Did you get the letter in Bogotá?'

'No, it was forwarded to me in Boston. I thought it was a wonderful letter and showed it to all my friends there. Apart from being enthusiastic it gave a good breakdown of the situation, showing how, despite the many mistakes, major gains had been made. Antonio was the only one to remain unmoved;

147

he's sceptical about everything except his business deals.'

'What's Antonio like?'

'The kind of person whose characteristics are not suffi-ciently well-defined for you to give a description of him,' Irene replied after stopping to think for a moment. 'But he's not so ill-defined that he's invisible either. I don't know how to answer you. Probably the only person capable of giving a witty description of him would be Luisa.'

'How does Luisa come into it?'

'She met him once when she came to Buenos Aires and stayed with me.'

'So you went on seeing Luisa after the night we all got arrested?'

'Yes, but only from time to time. We also exchanged the occasional letter; and then there were the two days I've just mentioned, which we spent chatting like you and I are doing now. After that I lost track of her; didn't I say I didn't even know she was in Lyons? Anyway I'm always on the move and Luisa's not the sort of person who's prepared to follow on anyone's heels, unlike you.'

So the arrest at Luisa's house had made more of an impact on her than she would ever have guessed. How amazing that she should have remembered more details about the house than Dolores herself; she, for example, had never registered how soft the cushions were on the velvet sofa in Luisa's dining room, nor had she seen the chairs lined up against the near wall, nor even noticed the curtains about to fall down. What she did remember was that sitting next to Irene had sent her into a strange trance, and that they'd had a long private con-versation in which she, who was not expansive even with Enrique, had told her personal anecdotes, secret details of her life. She had a gift for getting people to talk to her, there was no doubt about it! And Dolores would have gone on talk-ing for ever if only to retain the image of her looking into her eyes, gently but firmly, in rapt attention, ready to dispense whatever comfort was required. If it hadn't been for Luisa's apparently crazy gesture of getting on to the table to start reciting, which didn't surprise Dolores particularly, being just the latest item in the inexhaustible repertoire of eccentricities which Luisa loved to display on every occasion, she would never have taken her eyes off that sympathetic face. This time, however, she realised intently that Luisa's gesture was not gratuitous. What went wrong? She shuddered when she saw the Commissioner of Police appear in the doorway to the next room. What was he doing there? Then she remembered Luisa insisting that, if she invited him to the party, they would have a foolproof alibi. But she looked in his face and realised there had been a hitch in Luisa's carefully laid plans for the night. The night of the day when everything began in earnest and everyone was forced to take a stand. It was at that point that she heard the sound of a key turning in the door to Luisa's flat, and Juan came in, ashen-faced. She doesn't want to remember what happened after that. Surely she's not going to go over it all yet again? If only there were a God capable of protecting her from the implacable curse of memory, she'd be on her knees before his image begging to be spared. But who would grant her oblivion? Who would be prepared to extend such mercy? There's nothing for it, best to get it over and done with as quickly as possible by starting at the point when the Commissioner held out his hand to Luisa to help her down from the table, and she, glaring at him, leapt down ignoring his outstretched hand. A purple flush spread over his cheekbones. He must have realised then and there that his fate was sealed. Luisa would never forgive him his act of treachery; arresting her friends in the middle of her party, in her own house, that was going too far. The Commissioner must have thought that no more would he awake to the sound of the Siamese cats purring on the pillow, watching her sail into the room in her faded pink or mauve lace dressing gown, bearing a silver tray with a pot of coffee. He'd succeeded in rounding up the group that was robbing him of his sleep at night, but at the cost of securing his personal downfall, for to lose Luisa was a loss indeed: the end of the world of fantasy, magic and glamour which only she, with her years of experience, could open up before him. As she recalls the image of the Commissioner standing with his hand outstretched, the girl thinks that that night was the beginning of the end for everyone: for Luisa, for the wretch she'd kept in her bed to cover her tracks, for Enrique, for Juan. Even for Néstor and Flaquita, for what had they gained from saving their skins in order to bring up their son in this dump of a country? Even for Irene. Hadn't she once said in a letter that it was that night that opened her eyes politically, that made her start establishing contact with leftwing groups, which in turn had given her son the idea of going to Chile? And it was because he was in Chile, because he'd found the new, liberated utopia of his dreams, that his mother was now waiting in agony for news and he was probably dead like so many others, with no means of identification, no way of knowing how or where. 'The sadism of the media is plumbing new depths of refinement,' she thought. 'Wasn't it yesterday I heard it announced on the radio that the River Mapocho is thick with bodies and people are crowding the bridges to count them as they drift underneath?' Stop it! She had to reject that image of the Mapocho flowing with blood. No more dead bodies, I beg of you! She flashed back to the image of Luisa standing on the table, reciting. She'd been struck by the vigour and suppleness of her body, in her tight satin gown with shoulder straps. At first she felt like laughing out loud at the sight of her ridiculous antics as she pranced around the table, watching her steps so as not to fall off, reciting something totally unintelligible. She couldn't understand how such pranks had enthralled her in her childhood. She looked at the actress sitting next to her and again nearly burst out laughing at the sight of her gaping mouth, as the hostess went on declaiming absurdly on top of the table. Then she noticed the look of anxiety on Irene's expressive face; it was only then when she followed the line of her gaze that she spotted the Commissioner of Police. Irene had apparently been quick to realise that something sinister was going on under the tragicomic surface. Why hadn't she told the police who she was when they were dragged out of the flat? It would have been enough for her to give her name and the Commissioner would have fallen over backwards with apologies. 'She chose to go to prison with us,' the girl thought. 'She chose to come with us.' Was it an indication of a sense of loyalty on her part, or of a love of adventure? Though it has to be said that at the time no one took it all that seriously, it wasn't the first or last time they'd been bundled into a police van to spend the night in prison. It was true that things were getting tougher all the time, but Luisa was a genius at pulling strings; she was bound to get away with it this time as she had in the past. Anyway, going to jail was always exciting: one's initial fear always gave way to a deep-seated, glowing tingle of heroism. Had Juan managed to behave according to instructions? Dolores reflected that when the police extracted a confession out of you by beating you up or keeping you standing for hours on end, you were bound to invent it all because no one knew what was going on outside his own limited sphere of action; you knew what your orders were, but you didn't know the first thing about what other people were doing or what the next step would be. Wasn't it enough to have faith in the final objective of the struggle? A new life for people, free from humiliation and injustice and repression; her heart swelled with emotion. But at the same time she was troubled by the niggling memory of the hours spent standing in the open courtyard, and broke out into an anxious sweat. She also reminded herself that they were training people in the latest torture methods, but that was unthinkable in this sleepy backwater devoted to sheep-shearing and cattle-raising. The reassuring face of Judge Palau, who her father was always going on about, flashed up in her mind. The judge had an august, sweeping brow and twinkling, observant eyes; the true image of justice. No, as long as people like Judge Palau were around, electric torture would remain unknown in Uruguay. And anyway, if your local policeman knew you personally, how was he going to give you electric shocks? Such thoughts reassured her as the police van drove through the streets; but she couldn't stop shaking. Would she be capable of resisting torture? No, she'd blurt everything out with the first electric shock. Death was okay, but pain was another matter; or so she felt at the time. Of course the death she had in mind was completely unreal, a romantic invention, for what healthy twenty-year-old thinks about what it really means to die? The actress's hand on her knee jerked her back to her senses. She'd ended up sitting opposite her, with Enrique on one side and Juan on the other. Their knees kept knocking against each other. She was so lost in her thoughts that she had to make an effort to remember who she was and what she was doing there. The vision of that medieval pageboy dressed in pastel colours, banging her head mercilessly against the side of the police van whenever the driver hurtled — deliberately — over a pot-hole, was completely surreal. But the comforting touch of her hand helped her regain a sense of reality and again she found herself basking in the warmth of that encouraging smile. Then they went into the police station and lost sight of her. They were hustled off to the cells, she was left standing in front of the desk of the inspector on duty.

'It all began with her arrival.' The idea obsessed her and she couldn't get it out of her head. The only thing planned for that day was the demonstration in protest at the killing of a student, and all of a sudden, before they knew where they were, they found themselves in the middle of a blood-bath and discovered, too late as usual, that the enemy, less innocent than they'd thought, had been banking on that war as an excuse to seize power and had armed itself to the teeth, ready for a fight to the death. The enemy knew they were a bunch of mixed-up teenagers who, if pushed, would play the role of martyr to the cause; and they knew that the time had come to start systematically weeding out those improbable avenging angels. They were not the dull-witted brutes, deadened by routine, they'd taken them for; on the contrary, they were the all-knowing. When the avenging angels on this side of the River Plate started to drop like fruit ripe for the picking, their counterparts on the other side of the river took up the same ardent, desperate struggle. Had it been the product of desperation or an error of judgement? At this stage in the proceedings it would be ridiculous not to admit that there had been errors of judgement, but Dolores refused and would go on refusing to write it off as a mistake, as if it were a simple matter of missing your target or coming up with the wrong solution to the problem, when so many people had given their lives. And anyway, you could argue a case for almost anything being right or wrong, depending on your point of view. Hadn't the founder of the nation Artigas, whose Tupamaro soldiers had played such a vital role in the independence struggle, been regarded in his day as an outlaw, and wasn't he now claimed equally by right and left? Who decides when the outlaw becomes a hero, or vice versa? Nor would she let the other members of the group talk in terms of having made a mistake, for that was the argument used by people like Néstor and Flaquita to justify their desertion. When they let Néstor out of jail, the two of them kept going on and on about it, as if to convince themselves. Well, they'd made a mistake, we'd made a mistake. So what? To be honest, it was a logical enough thing to say in the circumstances. It let them off the hook, and their former comrades stopped having anything to do with them. Dolores might think it wasn't worth being cooped up in a dreary office all day just to eke out a meagre living, but no doubt Néstor and Flaquita thought otherwise, apart from the fact that there was a sickly little boy with a wizened face involved. At this point in the argument Dolores always got bogged down. She despised them and felt sorry for them at the same time. And it wasn't just the two of them, but the hundreds of other people, maybe more, who felt the same way. Flaquita got a job as a shop assistant when they sacked her from her office job, and every time someone came into the shop she would look up in terror. Fortunately for her, the shops in Montevideo were deserted nowadays, so she could spend hours staring blankly out of the window, her hands clasped behind her back. Dolores suddenly remembers how she met them in the street. Néstor had his arm round her and they both looked worried and depressed. She'd felt sorry she'd dismissed them as traitors. What they'd betrayed was hardly a big deal, after all. She couldn't bring herself to condemn them for the sole crime of wanting to stay alive and never more to have to spend days on end shivering with cold in a courtyard, not even being able to shift from one leg to the other without a kick in the shins, or to have to lie flat on their faces on the filthy, freezing floor of a prison cell. That evening, she'd discussed the matter with some other members of the group, and had pleaded on Néstor and Flaquita's behalf. They'd told her she was weak-minded and sentimental; what else could you expect from someone who wrote poetry? She sighed. Her head was spinning with memories after the conversation with Irene. There was no way she could stop them. Seeing her had stirred up all the emotions she'd been struggling to keep in check.

The bus pulled slowly into the terminus in the city centre, braking loudly. The driver lifted the hand brake and, without moving from his seat, took his provisions out from under the seat and went back to sipping his maté with relish. As she got out he didn't so much as give her a look, despite the fact that she'd been the only passenger to travel the whole length of the route. The girl landed on the pavement, inhaling the cool, night air. She was glad to have got home late, that way her parents would be asleep and wouldn't bother her with questions. At least she'd managed to get away from them for the whole of Saturday, and there was only an irretrievably dull, dismal Sunday left to get through. She'd make some excuse about having to get back to her rented room in the evening, and then she'd be rid of them and could forget all about their dreary existence for five whole wonder-

154

ful days.

She had to go right across the middle of the square, which wasn't much fun in the dark. But the gleam of the paving stones gave off just enough light for her to see where she was putting her feet, and at least there was no sign of anyone around waiting to stop her and ask to see her papers. No khaki army jeeps, either. 'And what's happened to all the police vans?' she thought automatically, seeing nothing stationed on the street corners. Unless they were lurking, as was their wont, in the inner courtyard of the Central Bank, ready to shoot off as soon as they received orders to go into action. This total absence of noise and people in a city under seige was strangely terrifying. She felt like running across the square but thought twice about it and set off at a brisk walk, trying to make as little noise as possible so as not to attract the attention of some soldier posted in the dark with his machine gun at the ready. Shoot first and ask questions later was the motto the loyal servants of the nation had borrowed from the banana-republic dictators who once upon a time they'd mocked. 'Once upon a time when you used to be able to criticise people,' she thought. 'Even people in uniform. How things have changed.'

As she turned the corner of the Calle Andes, the cold wind blowing from the waterfront blasted her in the face, making her squint and lose her balance. She'd been very sorry to leave the house near the cemetery, she didn't quite know why; perhaps because of her horror irrevocably inherited from her parents. It was just as well the owner of the house had claimed it back before she was arrested, or else they'd have blamed her for that too, no doubt. It had been a terrible upheaval for her parents to have to move after so many years but, surreptitiously and imperceptibly, her mother had managed to recreate the former darkness by keeping the shutters of the windows overlooking the river permanently bolted, insisting on the need to keep out the wind and the damp, which now took over the fiendish role attributed to the sun in the previous house. When she got to the doorway her teeth were chattering, despite the fact that it was well into spring; by the time she'd got from the front door, which she bolted behind her with a heavy iron bar in accordance with her mother's weekly exhortations, to the glass door at the end of the entrance hall, she'd managed to get her breath back. She leant against the wall, looking up, as she always did, at the skylight. She liked that skylight way above her head, with the yellowy light that shone through it in the day giving the ageing walls a velvety texture, and the sudden flickers that flashed across it at night. The entrance hall was a kind of no-go-area between the army lying in wait out in the street and her mother spying on her from the glass door. On the Saturdays when she got home early, she would see her shadow behind the muslin curtain, and her heart would start to flutter. At least she'd be asleep at this time of night. The walk from the front door to the other end of the entrance hall, broken by the fond gaze up at the skylight, always gave her time to ask herself whether what she felt for her mother was hatred or pity. This time she felt utterly miserable at the thought that she hadn't managed to buy her the television set; she was hoping that watching TV would act as an outlet for the strings of complaints endlessly muttered in the darkened rooms. She looked at the glass door ahead of her, its rounded mouldings, the gathered muslin curtain, the brass doorknob polished like a mirror. She took one last lingering look up at the iron ribs of the skylight. It was as black as ink. She inserted the key and turned the doorknob. She sniffed, trying to work out what the smell reminded her of; it was like a mixture of mothballs and damp. She groped for the felt skates with her feet and automatically boarded them. She slid effortlessly down the corridor, gliding to a halt at the second door on the right where they'd installed her old wooden bed, painted sky blue, still covered with worn transfers, that was now so small for her she had to sleep in a fetal position. They'd reconstructed her bedroom exactly as it had been when she was a child, not wanting to accept the fact that she no longer lived at home. She switched on the light trying not to make a noise, and a dim yellow halo appeared round the chintz lampshade. 'Twenty watts,' she thought venomously. 'It can't be more than twenty watts. Why does the same thought have to come into my head every single time I switch the bloody thing on?' She switched it off and curled up in bed without bothering to get undressed, trying to avoid the touch of the candlewick bedspread. She was still trying to get comfortable when she felt some hand poking her in the dark. She leapt out of bed, but the cold, wrinkled hands kept groping after her till they finally seized hold of one of the lapels of her blazer and started to tug at it. She tried to fight her way to the light switch and, when she finally managed to turn it on, was confronted by her mother's face, closer to her own than she'd ever seen it before. Her face was sallow and worn, her eyes deep-sunk. Was that what her mother looked like? She couldn't take her eyes off her mouth, which looked older than the rest of her face. Hundreds of tiny wrinkles converged on her pinched lips. She felt a wave of pity for that parched skin, like a crumpled piece of paper, and turned her head away.

'What's wrong now?' she managed to get out.

'Your father's died.' Her mother's lips barely moved as she whispered the words, but then she opened her mouth wide and started to screech.

Dolores listened to her mother's shrieks, not registering the meaning of the words, laboriously going over them in her head: 'Your father's died,' 'Your father's died.'

She heard herself saying out loud: 'What do you mean? What do you mean? What do you mean, my father's died?'

She needed to know the exact meaning of every word, but her mother, after studying her amazement for a second, started to assail her with the usual string of recriminations. She was astonished to find herself totally unmoved by her mother's abuse. All she wanted was to know what had happened. Please God, make her shut up and tell the story from beginning to end! As she addressed her plea to some unknown God, she knew it would not be granted and that she was expected to follow the usual incomprehensible logic: her father had died because she, Dolores, had killed him. Everything else was subordinate to that repeated phrase; her father had been destroyed by the shame she'd brought on the family; he'd been destroyed by losing his friends; he'd been destroyed by his daughter's ingratitude if you could use the word 'daughter' to describe the stranger who only came to see them once a week out of a sense of obligation and never brought them anything. 'The TV! Why didn't I get the TV?' the girl thought frantically. So her father had died on Wednesday—'Thursday, Friday, Saturday,' she made a mental count—of a heart attack. He'd been in the middle of eating his soup and his head had slumped slowly forward, narrowly missing his plate. And her mother was all alone as usual, and had had to rely on the neighbours to help her organise everything: the wake, the funeral.

She wanted to ask some questions but her mother went on upbraiding her, till finally she broke away from her horny grip and turned on her screaming why hadn't anyone told her, why hadn't someone thought of coming to tell her. But her mother had obviously anticipated that line of attack and had her counter-attack ready up her sleeve, because without a break she went on shrieking that she didn't even know where her daughter lived because she'd never so much as thought of taking them to see her new home, she was obviously ashamed of them but that made them quits because she'd made them feel like dying of shame what with everything that had happened. And now her father really had died of shame because she . . . ; and off she went again.

Dolores sat down on the edge of the bed. She stretched out a hand and traced round the edges of a sticker. A tiny, smiling figure in a straw hat was clutching a basket of flowers. The flowers were worn away in the middle, with a patch of sky-blue paint showing through. There was one all-pervading thought in her head: the need to get out of that house. 'I'm getting out of here,' she muttered, 'I'm never coming back, I never want to see her or hear her voice again.' She leapt up, picking up her bag on the way out, and ran down the corridor. She calculated quickly: 'She'll never catch me up by the time she's stopped to climb on the felt skates.' She left the glass door open behind her, cleared the three steps at a bound, ran down the hall and unbolted the door, also leaving it swinging ajar. 'She'll be too scared to go to the front door to bolt it. She'll be terrified out of her wits.' That vindictive thought cheered her up, but she felt her eyes brimming with tears. 'That's how old ladies get killed in the movies,' she thought as she ran back to the square. 'Someone sneaks in the front door and stabs them to death.' Her hatred was so monstrous and painful it made her heart ache. She would die of heart failure like her father, except that she wouldn't almost land in a plate of soup. She realised that she'd previously failed to register the grotesqueness of that detail. 'I bet it wasn't like that at all,' she thought. 'I bet she made it up to belittle him even in death.'

She came to a halt, panting, as she came out into the main square. And where did she think she was going? She realised that, without having formulated the idea consciously, she was retracing her steps in the hope of catching the last bus back to the beach. She had to see her again, come what may. She had to sit beside her and tell her the whole incredible story; she absolutely had to get her to explain what happens when your father dies, what are you supposed to feel, what do you do when you're in mourning, how does it affect the way you feel about the world. Or to reassure her by telling her that nothing happens, that the other deaths in her life were the important ones, not this one. But more than anything else, Irene had to take her by the hand to help her once more go down this tunnel leading to death, greet it with respect, drink it in through the pores of her skin, her veins, the marrow of her bones, till it suffused every inch of her body. Her entreaty took her aback: was that what she'd done with the other deaths? She'd have to ask Irene that too; if only she could turn her into an open plain, in the midday sun, everything in her life would become clear! She broke into a run, throwing all caution to the winds. Blind and deaf, mindful only of her desperate need to project her anguish on to someone else.

She came across no one on the way. Thank God for that deserted city, at least the violence had one good side to it. The bus was standing at the terminus, purring gently like a decrepit cat. When she went up to the driver to check the time of departure, she discovered it was the same one as before. He was sipping his maté with relish, eyes half closed. When he noticed her in the open doorway he jumped and gaped at her for a second, and she detected a flicker of suspicion on his face. 'Don't say he's going to get out and report me,' she thought for one awful moment. These days any trivial act, such as taking the same bus twice, especially at this time of night, was liable to be regarded as highly suspicious. Nothing paid better than giving information to the police, and everyone knew it. She fancied that the man was looking at her with the same covetous expression as her neighbours, the milkman, the son of the family in the boarding house, the newsagent. An expression where you could invariably read the same unspoken question: how much could I make out of her? If the driver read her thoughts, she was lost; but he looked out of the window, gave a quick glance at the deserted street outside, and gave her a curt, reluctant reply. Then he let out a sigh and went back to the complicated operation of stowing his thermos and maté under his seat. He consulted the timetable and, taking his time, made ready to start out on his bumpy journey.

Dolores climbed in and took a seat at the back of the bus, next to the exit, doing her best to avoid attracting the driver's attention, despite the fact that he kept taking the odd look at her in his rearview mirror.

The light inside the bus seemed even more gloomy than before. She felt a dull ache in her head; she leant forward to rest it on the metal handrail and felt a temporary sensation of relief. Her father's death, her mother's shrieks, the fight in the dark in the house in the Calle Andes, all seemed more and more unreal. Could it really all be true and could things really have happened in such a melodramatic way, like something out of a Gothic novel? She tried to conjure up in her mind the moment when her father's head nearly landed in the plate of soup. That couldn't be right, the shrew must have made it up. He must have died in his armchair, reading the paper; or maybe the heart attack had caught him as he was going down the corridor and he'd managed to crawl to the bedroom door and slump against it. In what film . . .? Or maybe he'd got out of bed to go for a pee and had dropped dead on the spot. But as she evoked these imaginary deaths she realised she couldn't for the life of her remember her father's face. The face she saw was that of Karl Malden or that other ageing TV actor whose name escaped her. It was useless, his face was a total blank. Did he have a moustache? Had he had one once and later shaved it off? A tremendous effort of concentration brought back the image of his spectacles, because it annoyed her that one of the earpieces was broken and tied together with string, but she didn't see them on her father's face but lying around on some piece of furniture, which always provoked interminable recriminations from her mother about his untidiness and how she had to do all the housework, etc. She felt it was a kind of betrayal to have died like that, without allowing her to see what his face was really like; that must be what wakes were for, so the bereaved could look at the face of the deceased in his coffin for the first time. It was the last chance to get acquainted with a face that previously had been unknown and that was why they hovered over the coffin like vultures, memorising the features of the deceased with painful astonishment. And that's why Enrique's mother refused to give her son up for dead; she'd never seen him lying still in his coffin, decked out ready to be studied and surveyed at length. (In fact, she's always said as much with that nervous smile of hers, as if apologising in advance.) And now it's Dolores's turn to demand to see her father stretched out in his coffin so she can go on looking at him with more curiosity than grief, it has to be said, in order to commit his face to memory, compare it with her own, work out similarities and differences, and discover why that face had previously been invisible to her. Invisible, forgettable, non-existent. While the nurse's face is engraved in her memory for ever, despite its lack of any clear individuating feature. But there it is, one eye slightly smaller than the other, fleshy lips, an ugly wart just above her upper lip, podgy cheeks, greying hair. And how did she know it was a little girl? She can't bear to think of the nurse looking at the fetus's face, but she can't stop thinking about it either. Her father, herself, his daughter, three generations of invisible people. The thought of her daughter takes her back to the other people who have died and, with a shudder, she suddenly realises she's not seen any of them dead. Neither Andrés nor Enrique, who she knows are dead for sure. And what about Juan? She can't bring herself to contemplate the sight of Victoria's corpse in a coffin. 'In this war the dead are invisible,' she mutters silently, hoping the driver won't notice she's talking to herself. Apart from that of Andrés, she doesn't even know where the other bodies are. 'Was it Enrique's body that they buried and Luisa marked with a stone? Or that of some stray dog?' The ghoulish parade of dead bodies starts up again. 'Dear God, is there no end to it, no rest for the disturbed imagination? At the end of the day our fate is to go for months and years from office to office reclaiming corpses as if they were suitcases. But when it's a body that's involved, no one will give you any information; or else, to fob off a hysterical relative, they'll hand over a tiny coffin with any old thing inside.' As had happened in her case. She started to count up to a hundred again to drive out of her mind the image of a dog rotting in Enrique's coffin. 'So where's Enrique then?' She cursed her father for dying and setting in motion this danse macabre always lurking in the wings.

Her head was throbbing violently just above her eyes. What would Irene say when she showed up at the door at this late hour? What with one thing and another, over three hours had elapsed. She'd probably be in bed by now. Would she finally see her radiant smile cloud over? She closed her eyes and a wave of tiredness swept over her; she could feel tears welling up in her eyes. Don't say she was going to cry, that was all she needed. But as she fought back the tears, she couldn't help wondering whether the mere fact of going on living wasn't superfluous, or simply one awful, big mistake. She felt incredibly sorry for herself. She would have given anything to be lying in bed, any bed, anywhere, except of course for the sky-blue painted bed at home, and to be able to wallow in self-pity. On second thought, her bed in the boarding house wouldn't do either; almost every evening that horrid little boy would open the door surreptitiously and peak wide-eyed at the woman lying on the bed with her hands behind her head, fully dressed and with her shoes on, one foot resting on the other, staring at the ceiling. Dolores never lowered her gaze but she knew the little brat was there and felt an intense hatred for him, but didn't know how to frighten him off and teach him a lesson. One of these days he'd get a good hiding. It seemed that she'd have to invent a new bed, because the ones she had . . . Perhaps at Irene's? Hadn't beds been the subject of the conversation they'd had the night they were arrested? How amazing it was that Irene should have remembered such details! She felt touched yet again by the warmth of that memory, offering its protection like a womb. Her head lurched forward and she leant it against the window to steady it against the jolting of the bus.

She was walking across a big room she didn't recognise; but then she was reassured by the familiar sight of the mauve lampshade on its coiled bronze stem. So she'd got there after all, though she hadn't expected to find so many people. She was puzzled that on the one hand the room seemed packed with people, but, on the other, she couldn't work out who any of them were. She moved forwards but the room turned into a slope at the end of which there seemed to be a garden. The worst of it was the constant toing-and-froing of the people

163

who kept blocking her view of the recess by the door. There were the bookcases and there was the recess by the door, so there was no doubt about it; they were in the house. The fact that Irene hadn't come to greet her filled her with dread; she must be watching her floundering in indecision, thinking yet again how inhibited she was, and so what? Aren't we all? A sudden flash of anger propelled her forward and she stretched out her hand to tap the man on the shoulder; but when she touched the cloth of his suit she found it was cold and clammy and prayed to God he wouldn't turn round. Now everyone was looking at her. She knew they were looking at her; she could feel the warmth of Enrique's understanding smile, and Andrés' ironic smile; but what most moved her was Victoria's smile, because she realised she was trying to encourage her, no matter how ridiculous a situation she'd got herself into. And where was Irene, who still hadn't showed up? She'd just gone past the bookcases when she spotted the elevator, with its door open. It was an antiquated elevator, the kind you find in a Paris hotel, but there was no shaft and inside it, squatting on the ground, was a three-year-old boy busy playing; he raised his head and looked at her, and she was rooted to the ground by his beauty. His white skin was offset by two enormous almond-shaped eyes, dark Indian eyes staring at her without blinking. He had thick, fleshy lips, parted in a smile such as Dolores had only ever seen on classical Greek statues. But what she was desperately trying to work out was who did the child look like and why was he there, at a clandestine meeting, when the police or the army might raid the house and carry him off? That must be what she had to warn them about, but she couldn't find them again in that maze where everything seemed to slope up and down. She thought she caught a glimpse of Victoria's golden hair but the woman turned round and her profile was that of somebody else, unless she'd got that thin in prison. The idea that Victoria's beauty could be so utterly destroyed weighed on her like a millstone. The best thing was to go back to the lift and squat on the floor with the little boy. It was then that they threw her to the ground and placed a foot on her chest again. It had yet to come down with its full weight; from her position on the floor she could see the boot very close to her face and tried to work out which bit of her body the man would start to jump on. It wouldn't be her belly, that was for certain; he wouldn't dare. The thought of how fragile her chest, her breastbone, her ribs were filled her with terror. But the man lifted up his boot and placed it on her belly. He put his whole weight on it and jumped in the air. She wanted to scream but there was no air in her lungs, all that came out of her mouth were whimpers and howls like those of an animal. Now she was crawling along the floor like a snail, leaving behind her a glistening red trail. She had to get to the garden but knew she would never make it. Something liquid was running down her body, they'd cut off her head with an ice-cold knife. The feeling of cold against her forehead woke her up. She raised her head, which had been leaning against the rim of the window, and looked up at the sky outside. Despite the total darkness overhead, she recognised the tall gateposts belonging to the former estate. Were they already turning into the avenue? Her head shot forward with the shock and banged against the glass, making what seemed to her a tremendous crashing noise. She sat up straight and looked at the driver; she could see his half-closed eyes looking in the rearview mirror. The bus was empty, had she been the only passenger for the whole of the long journey? She couldn't have been; the likelihood was that several people had got on and off en route. But she must have looked even more suspicious to the driver falling asleep like that. In a flash of terror, she remembered there was a police post just three blocks further down the avenue. He could stop the bus and turn her in... He must be furious with her for having stopped him sipping his maté.

She leapt up and pressed the bell. The driver looked startled, but pulled in at the stop. Dolores made off down a side street till the bus had disappeared from view, and then turned back on to the avenue and broke into a run, hugging

165

the privet hedges, praying there weren't any dogs on the loose. The avenue sloped downhill to the beach, fortunately, and if all went well she'd be at the house in a matter of minutes. Her legs kept seizing up unaccountably, making her stumble. 'I'm falling to pieces, perhaps my time is up.' But the thought, which usually she savoured, filled her with anguish. As she flicked back a strand of hair flopping over her face, so as to see better in the dark, she discovered her cheek was wet. She must have been crying, perhaps even sobbing, in the bus; she really was cracking up. 'I must cry out in my sleep at night, it must have become a talking point in the boarding house and that must be why that horrid little brat keeps peeking through the door at me.' She ran into some bushes and had to stop. She couldn't see a single light on. Were the people inside the houses groping their way around in the dark, or were they already tucked up in bed? She broke down into uncontrollable sobs, pressing her fists against her thighs; bloody people, how could they crucify us like that; they've massacred us, destroyed everything we had. She heard a dog start to bark furiously. The thought that at least dogs still had some fight left in them made her feel better for a moment. But the dog started to whine as if someone was hitting it, and suddenly went quiet. She strained her ears but could hear nothing. Panic-stricken by the silence, she started to run again and went on running non-stop till she got to the house.

There too everything was dark, but she went round the outside of the house and saw a light coming from one of the back rooms. She guessed she must be reading in bed. She sat down on the stone parapet to get her breath back and collect her thoughts. She took her handkerchief out of her pocket and furiously mopped her face. Now then, what were all these tears about? Her father? But she couldn't even remember his face! And yet that was the only ostensible motive. For months now she'd been living in a kind of limbo, throwing herself into her work, forcing herself to write, trying to steer clear of any upsetting emotion. Much the same as Flaquita, in fact; so much for her criticisms. The only disruption to her routine had been the news that Irene had arrived to stay in her house by the sea, and her decision to go and see her. Which was no reason for crying, quite the contrary. Perhaps that was precisely the problem and she was crying because she couldn't cope any more with even the slightest prospect of happiness. She suddenly remembered her dream on the bus and was surprised it hadn't been the usual nightmare. The nightmare element was there, of course; but she vaguely remembered having seen Victoria and other people smiling and also a child, the thought of which gave her an instant sense of relief. She looked at the house. It was the same house as in the dream, but it was different at the same time; the house in front of her was more sturdy and compact; she felt a burning desire to see light streaming out of the windows, for the shutters to be thrown back to let in the cool, night air so that other stray, lonely people like herself could catch a glimpse of the brightly lit rooms, the walls, the bookcases, the plants, the glowing lampshades, because that was what a home was, a light shining in darkness. But it wasn't enough to stay outside fondly gazing at the peaceful house, basking in its soothing caress. To want that was to want other delights that followed on in an unbroken chain; the light led you to the rooms, the rooms led you on to the pleasures of domesticity. And from there you could easily progress to the loss of fear; and having reached that point, you could take off, in a wonderful leap, bound for the ultimate goal of sensuality, passion and tranquility, all those things that enabled you to keep death at a safe remove. Stop it! She had to fend off such wild aspirations to happiness, just as other people bricked themselves up in their houses and plunged themselves into oblivion. It was what everyone did, even if they weren't aware of it; she must think twice before venturing on untrodden ground. Seeing her again had probably been a mistake, and now she was compounding it by running back to her in the hope of finding a meaning to her father's death, taking it for granted she would have all the answers. She was

dismayed to find herself thinking she ought to turn round
and go back the way she'd come. She started to shake with
uncontrollable laughter at the thought of getting back on the
same bus, with the same driver drinking the same maté; it
would be too much for him. But there wouldn't be any more
buses at this time of night, anyway. She'd have to walk all
the way back along the coast road which, in present circumstances, was tantamount to suicide. There wasn't the
slightest chance of her getting back alive and well to the city
centre with so many military patrols posted along the route.
They'd lost that too; the right to walk along the coast, to
go fishing in the harbour, to lie spreadeagled on the chalky
banks at the height of summer. There was no option but to
go up the steps and ring the doorbell, the sooner the better.
Irene was bound to take a sleeping pill last thing at night to
help her forget for a few hours about the bloodbath in Chile.
And then nothing in the world would bring her back to the
surface. Dear God, watch over me! It was the third or fourth
time she'd found herself repeating that senseless prayer. She
looked angrily up at the sky. It was impossible to imagine
a sky more dramatically black and yet, at the same time, less
threatening. 'Watch over me in my hour of need,' she murmured as she got up and went to the door. There was no bit-
terness in her voice as she surrendered helplessly to the worst
that fate could bring.

'What on earth are you doing standing out there? Come on
in, for heaven's sake! This very minute!'
    Did the words denote concern or anger? The girl couldn't
tell. She wished there were some way of finding out before
going into the house, but there wasn't. She slipped in through
the half-open door and the woman pulled it to silently. She
stood propped up against the wall, staring lamely at the books
on the shelves. She should never have come back! It was
always a mistake to try to repeat things. Irene would be
furious to find her back again at this time of night, when

168

she had so many other things on her mind. Only when she felt the woman's hand take her by the chin and tilt her face up towards her own did some life come back into her features; the hand's warmth and firm, friendly touch allayed her fears. They stood face to face, eyeing each other. The corridor lined with bookcases was completely dark except for a glimmer of light coming from the doorway that led to the bedrooms. The light was so dim Dolores guessed she must have draped something over the bedside lamp; she felt incredibly distressed by the thought that everyone had been reduced to taking precautions in order to make themselves invisible, as if such infantile measures were sufficient to put the brutes off the scent. She tried to brush the thought aside and concentrate on the present situation. She knew she ought to explain what she was doing here, but all she wanted was to stay huddled against the wall not saying a word, feeling the touch of the woman's hand smoothing her hair behind her ears, and hearing the words that came out of her mouth apparently without a trace of anger. Words to the effect that 'they'd better not stay there in the dark like zombies' and 'what a fright she'd given her, especially when she couldn't see a thing at night without her glasses and it had taken her ages to work out who she was through the peephole'. All she wanted was for that hushed voice that put everything back to rights to go on and on, but the memory of her mother's shrieks came back to her and she shuddered. The woman noticed her body quiver and thought she looked like a newborn animal thrown out in the cold to die. She slowly steered her to the sitting room where they'd spent the afternoon talking. She put her down on the sofa in the dark and went to sit at the other end, her knees tucked under her chin. But the girl neither moved nor spoke, mechanically fiddling with her hair. Irene looked to see if she was crying, but couldn't even hear her breathe. Oddly, she wasn't annoyed at her turning up so unexpectedly. On the contrary, she was glad to see her and felt that, with her return, the house had come back to life and, whatever the reason for her unexplained visit, it was a distraction from worrying about her son. As such thoughts went through her head and she started to relax, the girl stretched out an arm in the dark and fumbled on the coffee table for some matches. She found some and lit a cigarette; the woman stayed curled up on the sofa, making the most of her newfound sensation of relief. But the flickering light of the match gave her a glimpse of Dolores's face and she was horrified to see her expression of desolation. She felt guilty for thinking about herself all the time when the girl was obviously going through some kind of trauma, and leapt up trying to make amends. She squatted on the floor in front of Dolores and put a firm hand on her knee. 'Why don't you tell me all about whatever it is that's happened?' The girl felt like dissolving into tears on the spot; how could she explain it all in an orderly fashion without making a scene of it, which was something she hated? But before she'd found the answer her voice started to tell the whole story, in a flat, lifeless tone. As her voice droned on, she thought it all sounded incredibly banal and her father's death was utterly insignificant. And the woman's silence encouraged her to go on exploring that hideous tangle in which fear of life had become inextricably mixed with a feigned indifference to death; as she went on speaking, she was astonished to discover she was getting closer to touching that twisted knot and starting to unravel it. She was afraid the ends of the skeins would be stiff with dry blood but she no longer cared; all that mattered was to go on explaining her confused emotions, her insistence on keeping a reckoning of the dead and clinging to her unhappiness, till she got to the central question: how does one learn to live with this burden of sorrows? Or how does one peel it off, layer by layer like a blood-stained bandage, in the hope that the wound will have healed and one will no longer need it?

Dolores went on talking, and in the darkness failed to notice Irene pulling further and further away from her. Sitting on the floor, with her arms round her knees and her chin resting on them, the woman found herself listening to what for the last two weeks, since the news of the bombing of the presidential palace, she'd been refusing to hear and admit. The possibility of death was something she dismissed outright; even less could she accept that it might be necessary to learn to live with disaster. She refused to concede that such was the price she might have to pay for her cult of happiness. 'We'll get through it, we'll get through it; even Dolores has got through it.' She'd come through everything; and now she'd finally rid herself of her father, who she can't have cared much about. She was appalled that, having come through it all, she should want to return to the scene of the crime and keep raking it around, apparently prepared to pay the price, which was none other than the acceptance of defeat. She wanted nothing to do with that kind of masochism. The woman felt everything inside her rebel against the horrible insistence on returning to the past, for she never looked back and when she did it was only to embellish it to boost her ego. She desperately wanted her to stop, but at the same time felt obliged to respond with sympathy. Meanwhile Dolores, as she went on unravelling the knot that was choking her, interpreted the woman's silence as a sign of encouragement. But the latter had clammed up completely and a single thought was hammering in her head; don't listen to a word she's saying, ignore that doom-laden litany. Every time the girl stopped to have a smoke, the cigarette opened up whirling red holes in the dark.

'Now it's going to be my turn,' Irene thought, but she spoke the words aloud and for a second was startled to hear the sound of her voice.

'Today has been a strange day. I have to confess it never entered my head you might turn up in the afternoon, but I was even more surprised to discover how pleased I was to see you. I expect it's because I told you a whole lot of things I hadn't mentioned to anyone before, and also because in the course of the conversation we discovered we had more in common than we'd realised. For instance, you didn't know I was so close to Victoria's mother, nor did I know that you'd worked with Victoria. But apart from those coincidences, what's been bothering me since you left is why hadn't I talked to anyone before about my meeting with Elena and the whole horrible business of the Plaza de Mayo? Why hadn't I told anyone about it? I think I know why; because no one would have believed me, or, what's worse, if they had believed me they wouldn't have shared my feelings of anger and sadness. And that's what I can't come to terms with. The people around you, who give you a helping hand, work with you or go to bed with you, who were brought up to believe in the same things as you and who ostensibly still adhere to those ideals, now are capable of sitting back and watching you die without a trace of pity. They'd turn their thumbs down like a Roman emperor, giving the go-ahead for you to be torn limb from limb. That's what's changed: suddenly people who were incapable of killing a fly have lost all compassion. And when that happens, the minority, even if they're prepared to fight to the death, are destined to go under. It means genocide, do you realise that? The same as with the Jews and the Nazis. What's hard to work out is why you and I have ended up on the side of the victims, when we're not capable of killing a fly either; the difference in our case being, for good or for ill, who knows, that we don't go around talking about an eye for an eye and a tooth for a tooth or crying for blood. I don't know how you feel about things, but I often try to imagine what it must be like when some monster gives the order to shoot, or turns the electric current on, or plunges a girl's head into a bucket of excrement, and I'm filled with horror; but it would never occur to me to picture the scene the other way round, with me applying the electric current to the monster's testicles. Do you know what I mean?'

But Dolores said nothing. 'She must have fallen asleep,' she thought, but she could hear her breathing normally and anyway she felt an unstoppable urge to go on talking.

'The trouble is — and this may sound an awful thing to say — I don't find being on the side of the victims anything to be proud of. On the contrary I find it surprising and confusing, because I've never wanted to be on that side and I still can't accept it. And right now, when I don't have a clear picture of what's happening to my son in Santiago, I can accept it even less. I feel that . . .'

She fell silent, at a loss for words.

'The thing is, you never had a sound political education and you got mixed up in all this almost by accident, without really knowing what it was all about,' Dolores said. 'It's the same with a lot of people of our parents' generation.'

'Yes, I know, care and concern for our kids and all that. But my case isn't quite like that; that's too easy an explanation. In some respects that's the case with Andrés' father and, of course, Elena. But I feel that I've got there by an independent route. That I got involved on my own account, not because I approved of what you were doing — on the contrary, I thought most of what you were doing was pretty silly, not to mention ineffective — but because of the change I was just talking about: I mean the question of compassion and solidarity with others. Has the notion of pity been lost irrevocably? Because if it has, it means our society has lost all sense of humanity, that's what worries me.'

'What romantic concept of society are you talking about? It would make more sense if you saw this war as an all-out struggle for power. You can fit any amount of cruelty on the part of the victors into that scheme of things.'

'All right, you're simplifying the terms, putting the military on one side and, on the other, the armed struggle, the defeat of the revolution, total annihilation. I'm referring to the people in the middle. What about those who aren't actively involved, the onlookers, who incidentally are the vast majority? I can understand all the political explanations; conservative tendencies, latent fascism of the middle classes, systematic brainwashing, wanting to stay top of the pile, you name it. What I still want someone to explain to me is how a nation that supports the Society for the Prevention of Cruelty to Animals can have come to regard it as perfectly acceptable, indeed perfectly normal, for some brute to . . .'

She was going to say 'stick a pole up a girl's vagina till

it comes out the other end', because that true story obsessed her, but she fell silent and clutched her head.

'That kind of situation has arisen because most people think the victims are not human beings like themselves,' Dolores muttered. 'They never stop to think that the girl who's been tortured could be one of their daughters. It never enters their head to make the link. And when you get to the stage of regarding her as a member of a different species, a kind of poisonous reptile, the natural reaction is squash her without remorse. That's where the brutes in power have been so successful.'

'And what then? How can you undo the harm once it's been done?'

'You can't.'

'But what can you do to make people treat other people like human beings? I'm not letting anyone off the hook, mind you. Those who lose can be tried, sentenced or imprisoned; but for God's sake treat them like human beings!'

'You're back where you started, can't you see that? The brutes have been so successful because they've managed to convince the majority of people that, in addition to the human race, there exists another race that is not human, and which threatens their existence like aliens from outer space, just like in a science fiction movie. It's them or us. If that's how you see things, you consider you're acting in legitimate self-defence.'

'Legitimate self-defence against a little girl of three with a placard on her back saying "What have they done with my parents and grandparents?" . . . I saw that with my own eyes in the Plaza de Mayo.'

'She's not a little girl, she's the daughter and granddaughter of aliens from outer space; they'd squash her underfoot without batting an eyelid.'

'It's too awful for words,' Irene said quietly, after a pause.

They both fell silent. The woman calculated that she must have fallen asleep by now. She took her tightly clenched hands away from her knees and felt the knuckles tingle as the pressure was released. 'My whole body must be tied up in knots,' she thought. She stretched out the fingers of one hand and touched the girl's head. She had to make an effort to hide her feelings of hostility, and stop herself recoiling from the touch of that untidy, greasy hair or the smell of sweat and urine she sensed had clung to her from the prison cell. She slid her hand down to the back of her neck, but the girl's head fell forwards and buried itself in her lap. 'Now she's going to cry,' she thought, feeling more and more alienated. She didn't cry, however, but simply stayed in that position, as if the effort of talking had left her exhausted. She'd fall into a deep, sound sleep right away, as only young people can; the woman waited for a bit and, when she thought she could hear her breathing steadily, lifted her head out of her lap and slowly placed it on the floor. Then she groped for a cushion and put it under her head. She'd need a blanket for when it got cold in the early hours of the morning. As she opened the airing-cupboard door to look for a blanket, she imagined how soon she'd be doing the same for her son, as soon as he'd managed to get out that hell hole. The thought put her at ease and made her feel suddenly strong but, as always when she had such thoughts, the tears came pouring out. 'It's not me that's flagging, it's my wretched body.' She rested her forehead against the blanket, which was soft and fluffy. He'd be so happy to feel its downy touch after being exposed to the elements; but at that moment she realised that, if she ever did see her son again, he'd be a different person. Angry? Sorry for himself? Cynical? Whatever the case, a stranger, probably with a child. Again she was beset by the terrible realisation that there was no end to it and that things were happening in a real world, not an imaginary one, that foreshortened and distended time, and there was nothing she could do about it. The ground was starting to slip from under her feet yet again. She felt an irrational terror at the thought of having to live in this formless world where everyone was vainly clutching at shifting banks of sand. It wasn't fair, it wasn't fair; no one had prepared her for such a world.

She sighed and took the blanket into the sitting room where the girl was asleep on the floor; but as she was tucking her up Dolores took her hand and placed it between hers under the cushion. The woman let her hand lie there and sat cross-legged on the floor; she would watch over her patiently till she'd fallen fast asleep, in any case the night was always infinitely longer than her fitful sleep, plagued by nightmares. How many years was it since she'd last waited for her son to fall asleep before tiptoeing out of the room? Ten, fifteen? She felt dizzy at the thought of the past because, if at the time she'd insisted on cultivating it like a garden, now it felt like a steep slope. With her free hand she reached out for the lighter and cigarettes. She lit one up and inhaled slowly, savouring such tiny pleasures. It was odd but, with the girl at her side, she felt able to face the sleepless night ahead. As she slowly inhaled the cigarette, she began to recover some of her confidence in herself and in the future. Whatever might happen, she didn't feel like fighting; she let the drowsiness spread through her body.

The violent rapping on the front door woke them both at the same time. Dolores leapt up and started screaming hysterically. She ran to the back of the house with Irene running after her trying to calm her down, but she was completely beside herself, desperately searching for a way out or somewhere to hide. The woman finally managed to grab hold of her and push her into a corner, and they stayed crouching in the dark, like frightened animals, listening to the lock being blasted off the door and the boots stamping round the tiled floor in the sitting room. Then the noise got nearer and it sounded to them like a strange kind of rolling thunder, though it couldn't have been, but it blocked out every other sound, the wind blowing outside, their halting breath inside, the reassuring domestic noises, the hum of the refrigerator in the kitchen. The woman thought she might be able to control this frantic terror if she could focus on the sound of her own body, but for all her efforts at concentration she could hear nothing, not the slightest twitch of the pulse, not a single heartbeat. And in the total silence that other noise, cutting, merciless, grew and grew till finally it was all around them.

Jo Labanyi is Senior Lecturer in Spanish at Birkbeck College, University of London. She has previously translated Hernán Valdés, *Diary of a Chilean Concentration Camp*, Gollancz, 1975 and poems by various Spanish and Latin American authors for *Index on Censorship* in London and other magazines. She was the winner of the Spanish Section of the Translators' Association 1985 Short Story Translation Award for her translation of 'Chac Mool' by Carlos Fuentes.

Books from
Readers International

Sipho Sepamla, *A Ride on the Whirlwind*. This novel by one of South Africa's foremost black poets is set in the 1976 Soweto uprisings. "Not simply a tale of police versus rebels," said *World Literature Today*, "but a bold, sincere portrayal of the human predicament with which South Africa is faced." Hardback only, 244 pages. Retail price, US$12.50/£7.95 U.K.

Yang Jiang, *A Cadre School Life: Six Chapters*. Translated from the Chinese by Geremie Barmé and Bennett Lee. A lucid, personal meditation on the Cultural Revolution, the ordeal inflicted on 20 million Chinese, among them virtually all of the country's intellectuals. "Yang Jiang is a very distinguished old lady; she is a playwright; she translated Cervantes into Chinese...She lived through a disaster whose magnitude paralyzes the imagination...She is a subtle artist who knows how to say less to express more. Her *Six Chapters* are written with elegant simplicity." (Simon Leys, *The New Republic*) "An outstanding book, quite unlike anything else from 20th-century China...superbly translated." (*The Times Literary Supplement*). Hardback only, 91 pages. Retail price, $9.95/£6.50.

Sergio Ramírez, *To Bury Our Fathers*. Translated from Spanish by Nick Caistor. A panoramic novel of Nicaragua in the Somoza era, dramatically recreated by the country's leading prose artist. Cabaret singers, exiles, National Guardsmen, guerillas, itinerant traders, beauty queens, prostitutes and would-be presidents are the characters who people this sophisticated, lyrical and timeless epic of resistance and retribution. Paperback only, 253 pages. Retail price $8.95/£5.95.

Antonio Skármeta, *I Dreamt the Snow Was Burning*. Translated from Spanish by Malcolm Coad. A cynical country boy comes to Santiago to win at football and lose his virginity. The last days before the 1973 Chilean coup turn his world upside down. "With its vigour and fantasy, undoubtedly one of the best pieces of committed literature to emerge from Latin America," said *Le Monde*. 220 pages. Retail price, $14.95/£8.95 (hardback) $7.95/£4.95 (paperback).

Emile Habiby, *The Secret Life of Saeed, the Ill-Fated Pessoptimist*. Translated from the Arabic by Salma Khadra Jayyusi and Trevor Le Gassick. A comic epic of the Palestinian experience, the masterwork of a leading Palestinian journalist living in Israel. "...landed like a meteor in the midst of Arabic literature..." says Roger Hardy of *Middle East* magazine. Hardback only, 169 pages. Retail price, $14.95/£8.95.

Ivan Klíma, *My Merry Mornings*. Translated from Czech by George Theiner. Witty stories of the quiet corruption of Prague today. "Irrepressibly cheerful and successfully written" says the London *Financial Times*. Original illustrations for this edition by Czech artist Jan Brychta. Hardback, 154 pages. Retail price $14.95/£8.95.

Fire From the Ashes: Japanese stories on Hiroshima and Nagasaki, edited by Kenzaburo Oe. The first-ever collection in English of Stories by Japanese writers showing the deep effects of the A-bomb on their society over forty years. Hardback, 204 pages. Retail price $14.95/£8.95.

Linda Ty-Casper, *Awaiting Trespass: a Pasión*. Accomplished novel of Philippine society today. During a Passion Week full of risks and pilgrimages, the Gil family lives out the painful search of a nation for reason and nobility in irrational and ignoble times. 180 pages. Retail price $14.95/£8.95 (hardback), $7.95/£3.95 (paperback).

Janusz Anderman, *Poland Under Black Light*. Translated from Polish by Nina Taylor and Andrew Short. A talented young Polish writer, censored at home and coming into English for the first time, compels us into the eerie, Dickensian world of Warsaw under martial law. 150 pages. Retail price $12.50/£7.95 (hardback), $6.95/£3.95 (paperback).

Marta Traba, *Mothers and Shadows*. Translated from Spanish by Jo Labanyi. Out of the decade just past of dictatorship, torture and disappearances in the Southern Cone of Latin America comes this fascinating encounter between women of two different generations which evokes the tragedy and drama of Argentina, Uruguay and Chile. "Fierce, intelligent, moving" says *El Tiempo* of Bogotá. 200 pages. Retail price $14.95/£8.95 (hardback), $7.95/£3.95 (paperback).

Osvaldo Soriano, *A Funny, Dirty Little War*. Translated from Spanish by Nick Caistor. An important novel that could only be published in Argentina after the end of military rule, but which has now received both popular and critical acclaim — this black farce relives the beginnings of the Peronist "war against terrorism" as a bizarre and bloody comic romp. 150 pages. Retail price $12.50/£7.95 (hardback), $6.95/£3.95 (paperback).